What kids are saying about Cheesie Mack:

"Hey, Cheesie!!! I am a BIG fan right after reading your book
a few minutes ago. You and Georgie are awesome!!!"
—Max, Singapore

"Your book was amazilicious! I ate it right up!"
—Lila, New York

"I read the whole book in two hours, it was so good."
—Hunter, Texas

"I totally love your book! P.S. I love mack and cheese too!"
—Amanda, Wisconsin

"I can't wait until your next book."
—Liam, Alberta, Canada

"I loved your book! I just finished it and as soon as I did,
I ran to my computer and went on your website."
—Cara, Connecticut

"This is the best book I've ever read!"
—Michael, Illinois

"Cheesie Mack is the best!"
—Monica, Massachusetts

"Ronald Mack, you have grabbed my
funny bone and tickled it!"
—Tanvi, South Carolina

"Keep writing, Cheesie Mack!!!"
—Ella, California

READ ALL OF CHEESIE'S ADVENTURES!

CHEESIE MACK
IS COOL IN A DUEL

STEVE COTLER

Illustrated by Adam McCauley

A YEARLING BOOK

Text copyright © 2012 by Stephen L. Cotler
Front cover art copyright © 2012 by Douglas Holgate
Back and spine cover art and interior illustrations copyright © 2012 by Adam McCauley

All rights reserved. Published in the United States by Yearling, an imprint of Random House Children's Books, a division of Random House, Inc., New York. Originally published in hardcover in the United States by Random House Children's Books, New York, in 2012.

Yearling and the jumping horse design are registered trademarks of Random House, Inc.

Visit us on the Web! randomhouse.com/kids

Educators and librarians, for a variety of teaching tools, visit us at RHTeachersLibrarians.com

Visit Cheesie at CheesieMack.com!

The Library of Congress has cataloged the hardcover edition of this work as follows:
Cotler, Stephen L.
Cheesie Mack is cool in a duel / Steve Cotler ; illustrated by Adam McCauley.
p. cm.
Summary: The summer after fifth grade, Cheesie and Georgie go to camp in Maine, where they discover that they are bunking with the older kids and Cheesie must face off in a Cool Duel with dreaded Kevin Welch.
ISBN 978-0-375-86438-4 (trade) — ISBN 978-0-375-96438-1 (lib. bdg.) — ISBN 978-0-375-89571-5 (ebook)
[1. Camps—Fiction. 2. Contests—Fiction. 3. Maine—Fiction.]
I. McCauley, Adam, ill. II. Title.
PZ7.C82862Ch 2012 [Fic]—dc23 2011016921

ISBN 978-0-375-86395-0 (pbk.)

Printed in the United States of America

10 9 8 7 6 5 4 3 2 1

First Yearling Edition 2013

For my children and their partners,
from whom I continue to learn.
And for Ann.

Contents

Contents

CHEESIE MACK
IS COOL IN A DUEL

Who Wrote This Book . . . ?

I did. My name is Ronald Mack. But almost everyone calls me Cheesie Mack. Get it?

I'm eleven.

. . . and Why?

I wrote this book because everything in it happened to me, and it was terrific, scary, goofy, and weird, but not exactly in that order. I've already written the whole story you will read after you finish this chapter. And now I am doing this chapter last even though it comes first.

I call this the Preamble chapter because even though it's a word that most kids don't know, I think it's perfect. *Pre* means "before" and *amble* means "walk." So this chapter comes BEFORE you go for a WALK through the story of how I was *Cool in a Duel*.

If you've already read *Not a Genius or Anything*, which was the first book I ever wrote, then you already know that:

1. This book takes place the summer after I graduated from fifth grade.
2. I live in Gloucester, Massachusetts, with my parents and grandfather and one

older sister whom I call Goon (even though
her name is June) because she is usually
rotten to me. When my first book ended,
the score of the Point Battle between Goon
and me was 623–616, with her barely
ahead. I'll explain all that later, and you'll

3

have to read this book to find out who's ahead now.

3. I have a super-best friend named Georgie Sinkoff, who lives on the other side of the little creek behind my house. I have known him since we were really small.

4. When this book starts, Georgie and I are on a bus that is heading north to summer camp in Maine.

But if you didn't read *Not a Genius or Anything*, then you're reading my second book before my first one. Even though that's backward, it's probably okay. But you should know that:

1. I was the second shortest kid in fifth grade, but I grew over the summer, so now I'm the fourth shortest boy, and since two girls are now shorter than me, I'm the sixth shortest in sixth grade. So, since there are twenty-five kids in my class, 20 percent of them are shorter than I am. You can probably guess that there are lots of word problems in sixth-grade math.

2. I have brown hair, brown eyes, and three freckles on my nose. Georgie has reddish-brown hair, greenish-brown eyes, and cool glasses with bright red frames. He also has braces, which I may get later this year. He is the strongest and way tallest kid in sixth grade.

3. My ears stick out. (Even though I didn't want to, Georgie insisted that I mention this because he says it's the first thing people notice when they meet me. But once this sentence ends, you will see that I did not mention my ears even one more time in this book because no matter what Georgie says, my ears were not important to what happened.)

4. And, as you can tell, I like making lists.

I started writing *Cool in a Duel* one minute (not kidding!) after finishing *Not a Genius or Anything*. I am now in middle school, so it took me a long time to write this story because of all the homework. Just like my last book, this one is totally true. I did not make anything up.

I hope you like it. If you don't or do or whatever, please go to my website and tell me what you think.

Signed:

Ronald "Cheesie" Mack

Ronald "Cheesie" Mack (age 11 years and 2 months)
CheesieMack.com

Chapter 1

Lovey-Dovey Goon

QUESTION: What should a kid do when his evil older sister sneaks a half-melty chocolate bar onto his seat in the movies . . . and he sits on it . . . so when he goes outside after the film is over, people laugh at him because it looks like he . . . well, you know.

ANSWER: Wait three days until she's forgotten all about it . . . and then take advantage of the perfect opportunity to embarrass her back!

* * *

"Kevin's getting out of his mom's car," I whispered to Georgie. "Can you see Goon?"

"She's over there," he replied, pointing toward a

crowd of girls near the front of the nearest bus. "I don't think she sees him yet."

I switched the setting on Granpa's digital camera to movie mode.

It was the fifth of July, and we were scrunched down behind a car in a big parking lot just north of Boston. All around us, parents from Massachusetts, Connecticut, and Rhode Island were driving up and unloading kids and suitcases, sports equipment, backpacks, and other camp stuff. In a few minutes, we'd begin the four-hour bus ride from Boston to Camp Windward (boys) and Camp Leeward (girls), which are on the shores of Bufflehead Lake in central Maine.

"She's spotted him. She's waving," Georgie whispered again.

I peeked around Georgie. Goon had left her friends and was walking toward Kevin Welch, who is thirteen, an eighth grader, and my sister's so-called boyfriend.

"Let's move out," I whispered.

Actually, we didn't need to keep our voices low. The bus engines were running, kids were jabbering, and our targets (Goon and Kevin) weren't close. But if you're on a secret revenge mission to catch your sister saying something totally embarrassing to her jerky boyfriend, whispering is exactly right.

Bent over in a half-crouch, Georgie and I ran toward them, making sure to stay behind parked cars and groups of people. We hid behind one of the six buses, just a few feet away from Kevin.

Goon was getting closer.

I flipped out the camera's view screen, started filming, and edged my arm around the back of the bus. I moved my hand until I had Kevin and Goon in view.

"This is going to be such a great summer, Kev," Goon said.

"Uh-huh," he replied.

She reached out and took his hand. I started to chuckle, but stopped when I realized I was shaking the camera.

"Only bad thing is"—she reached for his other hand—"we won't see each other very much at all."

"Uh-huh," Kevin said.

She rocked their arms back and forth, kind of like she was dancing with him.

"Oh, Kevin," Goon said.

Georgie, staring at the camera's view screen over my shoulder, whispered in a Goonish voice, "Ohhhh, Kevin."

"Shhh! You'll get in the microphone," I warned.

"I'm going to miss you so, so much," Goon said.

This was perfect! Her face was all lovey-dovey. I couldn't help myself—I laughed out loud.

Uh-oh! The look on Goon's face suddenly changed from lovey-dovey to I'm-going-to-slug-someone!

I took off running. Goon pushed past Georgie and charged after me, but I am faster by far. Dodging kids and duffel bags and parents, I dashed to my bus and leaped up the steps. Goon followed me in, but by then I was all the way in the backest row. The camera was still recording, so I aimed it at her.

"Give me that camera!" Goon shouted as she stomped down the aisle toward me. Her mouth and eyes were pinched with anger.

"Girl on the bus!" yelled one boy.

Georgie appeared behind Goon. "Call the bus police!" he yelled.

"Alarm! Alarm! Alarm!" screamed another kid over and over.

Goon looked around at the dozens of boys who were now hooting and laughing at her. She turned red, spun around, shoved Georgie, and ran out.

It was a victory for me in the Point Battle, which is my secret way of keeping track of the war between me and my sister. Nobody—not even Georgie, and especially not Goon—knows anything about the Point Battle. Causing Goon to do something embarrassing when other people are around is worth four points. Her lead was shrinking. The score was now 660–657.

If you're good at math, you probably noticed the score's gone up a lot since my last book ended. That's because there have been lots of Point Battle events (like my chocolate pants!) in the days between then and this bus ride to camp. Because there was no school, the two of us had to be around each other a lot, so Goon was constantly attacking. She's older, meaner, and sneakier, so I had to be extra clever and vigilant (that means "watchful") just to keep the score close.

I put the Point Battle scoring rules at the back of this book in Appendix A.

An appendix is sort of like a chapter, but it's at the end of a book. An appendix is also some kind of thing inside your body. You probably know that, but do you know where it is? And do you know you have a philtrum near your nose? Or a tragus on each side of your head? There are all sorts of weird words for parts of

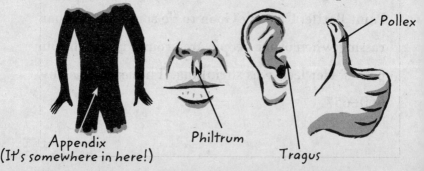

Appendix
(It's somewhere in here!)

Philtrum

Tragus

Pollex

the body. I stopped sucking my pollex (that's a thumb) before I was two. You can look these up on my website. I have a page that lists strange body-part names.

Lots more boys came onto the bus. It was getting loud with all the chatter, most of it about camp. I have gone to Camp Windward every summer since I was seven. If you like fun, it is the best place ever. Great friends, lots of sports, and plenty of adventures. I even saw a moose once. My grandfather is the camp director. At home I call him Granpa, but at camp everyone—even me—calls him Uncle Bud.

Since Granpa runs the camp, you might think I would get special treatment, but he is really strict about things like that. When I asked why, he said, "Fair-and-Square is my middle name" (which it isn't), and then gave me a squinty-evil-eye (which is a Mack Family Tradition that means the squinty-evil-eyer has a secret or is kidding or something). But I do get to be the first kid onto the bus, and I always take the backest row. Sitting there has several important advantages:

1. If you sit anywhere else, fun things might happen behind you, and you won't see them.
2. No one can sneak up on you.
3. Every other bench has only two seats. The backest has five, which means you can be with more friends.

I could hear and feel suitcases and stuff being loaded into the compartments under our feet. I leaned down and touched my sock. The five straws were there, right where I'd put them this morning.

Why did I stash straws in my sock? Only twenty minutes into last July's trip, while I was playing License Plate Alphabet Race against Georgie (the rules are on my website), a bunch of boys began zapping everyone with spitballs.

We were sitting ducks. The only thing we could do was duck behind the seat in front of us. We were ducking ducks. Every time we peeked out: ZAP! SPLAT! More spitballs.

This year I came prepared. If a spitball war started again, I'd be ready with:

1. Weapons—One plastic straw for each kid

in the backest row. I did not bring the flexible kind. Or the kind that come with juice boxes. Those are too skinny.

2. Ammo—Several sheets of paper. You tear off a piece, then chew it into a wad the same size as the inside of a straw. Several shots can be stored in each cheek, and lots more can be ready for action in your T-shirt pocket. It's better if you let them dry out before you put them in your shirt. I'm sure you can figure out why. (Do not use newspaper. It tastes terrible.)

3. Accuracy—Georgie and I had practiced at home. I am good, but he is unbelievably accurate. Any kid closer than four rows would be toast. At six rows, we had a fifty-fifty chance. At eight rows, who knows?

I began chewing paper and adding to my ammo supply. The bus was almost full. I was sitting right in the middle of the backest. Next to me on one side were Georgie and my camp friend Robbie Turner. Robbie's brother, Evan, also a camp friend, had his head down in the other corner of the backest playing a video game on his cell phone. Robbie and Evan are redheaded twins, but not the identical kind.

Camp friends are kids who do not go to your school or live in your town. You only see them during the summer, but you really like them, and you know them really well because you live in the same cabin with them for six weeks and eat every meal together and play games and lots more. It's one of the reasons why I love Camp Windward.

Georgie and Robbie were on their knees looking out the back window, making faces at kids and talking about using the batteries in Robbie's mom's hybrid car to power a laser gun you could mount on its hood.

Then disaster stepped onto the bus. It was Kevin Welch and his brother, Alex. Georgie and I were in fifth grade with Alex. He is, IMO, a worthless tattler and a twerpy jerk.

Alex walked toward the back of the bus, making fart noises at everyone. Then he spotted me and grinned as if I were his best friend.

Not!

He passed up lots of empty seats and, without asking, plunked down in the empty backest seat, the one I was saving for my camp friend Lenny Kalecki. I immediately pushed Alex back into the aisle and pretend-puked, but Kevin suddenly appeared behind Alex like a sea monster rising up out of the ocean.

Actually, that's not a bad description of Kevin. Like a sea monster, he is big, strong, green, and ugly.

I lied about the green.

"Your sister wants the camera. Hand it over," Kevin growgled.

(I made *growgle* up to fit with the sea monster thing. It's a combination of *growl* and *gurgle*. It's not a real word, but it *is* what Kevin sounded like.)

"It's Uncle Bud's," I said. "You'll have to ask him."

Kevin gave me a mean look, then walked away to sit with guys his age about five rows up. There will be lots more about Kevin in this book . . . almost all of it not good.

Alex just stood in the aisle, grinning stupidly.

I ignored him and passed out straws and paper to Robbie, Evan, and Georgie.

"What're these for?" Robbie asked.

"Operation Bus Blaster," I said. "You know . . ." I put a straw up to my mouth and pretended to shoot a spitball.

"Just in case," Georgie said to the other guys.

I started to put the two straws I was saving for me and Lenny back in my sock, but Alex grabbed one, laughed, and ran off to sit somewhere. Then I heard a loud "Wind-WHOOP!" and everyone turned to the front of the bus.

"Wind-WHOOP" is the unofficial official Camp Windward cheer. Lenny Kalecki had stepped onto the bus. He made up this cheer two years ago. Last year, the Camp Leeward girls got jealous and began yelling, "Lee-LOOP!" which I think makes no sense. On the last night of camp when we have a joint campfire, the two groups alternate cheering. It can get pretty loud.

Wind-WHOOPing and pumping his fist up and down, Lenny took a long time to get to the back of the bus. There were lots of high fives and knuckle bumps.

Then Granpa, who had been directing everything outside, blew his whistle (the kind basketball refs use). Lenny started Wind-WHOOPing again, and when I joined in, so did Robbie, Evan, and Georgie. Pretty soon lots of guys were Wind-WHOOPing.

I leaned over the kids in the seat in front of me and craned my neck out their open window. Granpa lifted both his arms into the air as the bus drivers took their seats and closed the doors. Then he blew three short blasts on his whistle and yanked his arms down. Immediately all six bus horns and all the parents' car horns started honking.

That's the way Camp Windward and Camp Leeward kids and their parents say goodbye to each other.

With maximum NOISE!

We do it every year.

I leaned back, pulled Granpa's camera out of my pocket, and with Georgie leaning over to look at it, replayed the video we'd shot.

I am a terrible cameraman. The image was all jumpy, Goon's face was all shadowy, and we could barely hear her saying, "Oh, Kevin . . ."

We didn't care. We all laughed. The summer was starting out great!

Chapter 2

Operation Bus Blaster

It was pretty noisy on the bus. Everyone was excited. I was smiling inside, just sitting in the

middle seat of the backest, my feet stretching out into the aisle in front of me, daydreaming about the next six weeks.

Here's why. The boys at Camp Windward get divided into two groups: Big Guys and Little Guys.

The Big Guys play different sports, like lacrosse and flag football, and have dances and stuff with Camp Leeward. The two groups don't see much of each other, except at campfires and meals.

Georgie and I have been Little Guys for the last four years. This year we'd be Little Guys again, but because we'd be in the eleven-year-old bunk, we'd be the *biggest* of the Little Guys, and that was why this was going to be our best summer ever. (I was actually still ten, but since my birthday would come on the last day of camp, that counted!)

Georgie and I terrifically love going to camp. But we almost didn't get to go this summer. If you read *Not a Genius or Anything*, you know why. If you didn't, I'm not going to give the plot away because you might read it someday.

For the first fifteen minutes on the bus, I was constantly watching out for incoming spitballs. But then Lenny began talking about his remote-control plane.

"It's awesome! Got a wingspan like this." He held his arms out wide and began talking about loop-the-loops and barrel rolls, and pretty soon I was completely interested and paying no attention to anything else.

That was when a spitball hit my arm.

I spun around, looking everywhere, but all heads were facing front.

"Guys," I whispered. "Don't look now, but the spitball war has begun. I just got hit."

Every one of them looked anyway. So did I. Alex Welch was looking back at us. He turned away quickly.

"Correction," I said. "This isn't a war. It's a one-man sniper attack. Everyone act natural. Lenny, let us know when to launch a counterattacking artillery barrage."

Barrage rhymes with *garage,* and means "a whole bunch of guns firing all at once." I love unusual words. Having a good vocabulary makes writing a lot more fun and gets me excellent grades on things I write for school. The first time I ever used the word *barrage* was in a report last year. I wrote: "I was attacked by a barrage of howler monkey screams long before I could see the primate cage." I got an A+ on my primate report. It's on my website. I'm assuming you know what a primate is . . . you primate!

A few moments later, Lenny whispered, "The target is definitely Alex Welch. He has a straw in his mouth. Okay, he's facing front now. Ready . . ."

I turned and aimed directly at the back of Alex's neck. I gave a quick look to both sides. Three other cannons were aimed at Alex. I moved a spitball from my cheek and tongued it into position just inside the straw.

"Aim . . . ," Lenny whispered.

I steadied my hand and drew in a big breath through my nose.

"Fire!"

Whoosh!

Splat! Splat! Splat! And splat! Four super-soggy spitballs smacked into the spitball sniper.

Alex spun around. "Quit it!" he yelped.

"You started it!" Georgie shouted back.

"We're even," I said. "Gimme back my straw."

Alex shook his head, then turned back around and began complaining to his brother. Kevin ignored him.

"Mission accomplished," Lenny said. "Cheesie's Operation Bus Blaster was a total success. Good shooting, gentlemen. Bull's-eyes all around."

After a while, the road signs indicated we were on the interstate going north through the tiny bit of New Hampshire that touches the Atlantic Ocean. I knew from experience that in a few minutes, when the bus crossed over the Piscataqua River Bridge into Maine, there would be a big cheer.

Because I liked the way it sounded (piss-CAT-uh-kwah . . . no giggling, please), I once looked it up, hoping it meant something like "shark-infested quicksand" or "don't eat the poisonous clams." Turns out it's a Native American word that means "branch of a river with a big current."

I could see the New Hampshire—Maine state-line sign coming up fast. Suddenly the whole bus exploded with loud screams. And at that exact moment, a spitball hit my chin. I couldn't believe it! There was Alex, straw in hand, grinning at me.

I yanked my straw out of my sock, tossed a bunch of T-shirt pocket spitballs into my mouth, and fired

back at him. Bad idea. I didn't plan. Alex ducked, and my shots missed him entirely. They went one row farther and smacked Kevin right in the cheek.

I might've been safe if I'd dropped my peashooter out of sight, but I was too stunned by my bad shooting. Kevin spun around, saw me with the straw still in my mouth, and jumped out of his seat. He stormed to the backest and stood in front of me.

Kevin's big. I'm small. But I wasn't afraid he was going to do anything to me. Kevin is way smarter than his brother. He did exactly what I thought he would do . . . which was even worse.

"Listen, Runt." He calls me Runt, which I hate, because that's what my sister mostly calls me.

"You"—he gave me a hard look—"have just bought yourself a summer of pain." He started to turn away, then looked back at me. "I'm gonna make sure of it."

No one made a sound as he walked back to his row. He tapped his seatmate on the shoulder, mumbled something I couldn't hear, then pointed at me. The other boy, a big guy named Ty who had been at camp for only one year and whom I had never really talked to, stared at me and smiled. It was definitely not a smile of friendship.

I looked left and then right at Georgie and my camp friends, Lenny, Evan, and Robbie. "Oh, great," I said. "Now I have camp enemies."

Chapter 3

The Greatest Camp in the Whole Known Universe

Three boring bus hours later we turned onto the road that leads into Camp Windward, and our boredom instantly disappeared.

As the bus bounced through the woods and over the hill and stopped in the parking area, every kid— me too!—was talking or yelling or both. Then Lenny began Wind-WHOOPing, so I instantly joined in and elbowed Georgie in the ribs to get his attention. Soon our row . . . then the rows near us . . . then the entire bus was Wind-WHOOPing.

It was great! Summer fun on Bufflehead Lake had finally begun. I had completely forgotten Kevin's threat.

Interesting fact: A bufflehead is a small black-and-white duck with a large head. The name is from "buffalo head." I put a picture of one on my website.

Even more interesting fact: There is a place in Massachusetts called Lake Chargoggagoggmanchaug-gagoggchaubunagungamaugg. It's true! Granpa took me fishing there. You can hear him pronounce the name on my website.

Boys and girls swarmed out of the six buses and joined the crowd of others who had driven up with their parents or came in buses from New York and New Jersey.

I'm sure I was grinning big-time as I looked all around. Here's what I saw:

1. Everyone was running every which way saying hello to camp friends.

2. Uncle Bud (I'm going to write his name that way when he's doing camp stuff, but he'll be Granpa when he's being my grandfather) was standing right in the middle of the parking area holding a battery-powered megaphone. He was trying to be all stern

and businesslike, but when he saw me, he gave me a squinty-evil-eye (which meant, "Aren't we going to have fun this summer?").

3. Parents were kind of standing around.
4. The drivers and the camp staff began unloading the bags and stuff from under the buses.
5. Deeb, my very smart springer spaniel, was zooming everywhere, sniffing everything, and getting patted and petted a million times.

Uncle Bud had brought Deeb to camp because my mom and dad went on vacation to Alaska. I'd get to play with Deeb whenever I wanted. Best of all, because the camp is in the woods, I would not have to clean up Deeb's you-know-what.

Uncle Bud lifted his megaphone and boomed, "Welcome, campers! Welcome to Camp Windward! Welcome to Camp Leeward! It's going to be a great summer. Parents, please say your goodbyes now. We've got a lot to do this afternoon before dinnertime."

Someone scooped me up and lifted me above his head. It was Scott Dutcher, the greatest counselor in the history of ever!

"Hiya, Cheesie!" he said, looking up at my grinning face. He pumped me up and down a couple of times like he was lifting weights, swung me down onto my feet, and then rubbed his knuckles across my pate. (If you don't know that word, you can find it on my body parts webpage.)

"I thought you weren't going to be at camp this summer," I said. (This was in my last book.)

"Changed my mind," he chuckled.

Lenny jumped onto Dutcher's back. "You gonna be our counselor again?"

Dutcher wiggled out from under Lenny and yelled over his shoulder as he jogged off to help unload the buses, "Abso-tootin-lutely!"

That was the best news! Lenny Wind-WHOOPed. Georgie was so happy he slugged me. Robbie and Evan did a crazy dance, almost bumping into Aunt Lois.

Aunt Lois is Granpa's ex-wife, but she is not my grandmother because she married Granpa when my dad was fifteen and got divorced long before I was born. It's complicated.

Aunt Lois owns both camps. She laughs a lot and is always cheerful. Uncle Bud is always grumpy, but I think that's mostly an act. Aunt Lois is totally artistic and creative. She makes every summer different. Here's how:

1. Before camp starts, Aunt Lois dyes two stripes into her hair, which is normally almost white. The stripes indicate what the team colors will be for Color War. This year her stripes were purple and orange.

2. One day—you never know when—is Strange Day. You don't know what to expect until she announces it at breakfast. Last year it was Sing-Only Day. No one, including the camp staff, was allowed to talk normally. At first it was embarrassing and hard, but by dinner, it was totally funny and fun.

3. Every year Aunt Lois puts up a new sculpture somewhere in camp. Last summer she attached one of those lawn gnome statues to the front half of an old rowboat, put it all on tall legs with a ladder up the side, and installed it as the lifeguard's chair on the beach where we swim.

Georgie and I were watching Dutcher unloading the suitcases two and three at a time when someone poked me in the neck. Hard.

It was Goon, my evil sister. "Kevin told me he is going to murder you."

I ignored her.

"He is definitely going to murder you."

"Then I'll be dead. Go away."

She didn't move. She stood way too close to me, grinning.

Goon and I have had an adversarial relationship for as long as I can remember. (Peter Pan and Captain Hook are adversaries. It's a high-class way of saying "opponent.")

Goon tried to poke me again, but I jumped away,

and she stumbled and fell. A couple of girls giggled, and Goon blushed. Four points for me! The score was now 661–660. I was ahead!

Since mostly the only times the Little Guys ever see the girls is across the dining hall at meals, summer camp is the one time of year when I have very little contact with my sister, so there was a good chance I'd be in the lead all summer. The last time I led, I was in fourth grade and the score was only 17–15!

Goon was gone for less than a minute when I heard another girl's voice. "Hello, Cheesie."

Georgie turned. I didn't. I knew who it was: Lana Shen, the girl from my fifth-grade class who all last year was always hanging around and talking to me.

"Hi, Lana," I said, still staring at Dutcher, not turning around.

"This is my friend Marci Housefield."

I turned a little bit. Lana was my size, but Marci was really tall, almost as tall as Georgie . . . and really skinny.

"I told her all about you," Lana said, staring at me.

Lana always stares at me. I don't know why, and

I have never asked because if I did, she'd probably tell me . . . and I don't want to know. So I just stared back without saying anything. Lana's hair is black and very shiny.

Just then Goon appeared again, leaned between us, and said, "Kiss, kiss," with lots of smooching sounds.

If I hadn't reacted, she would have gotten no points, but I instantly turned red. Four points for her. The Point Battle score was 664–661. I'd been in the lead for less than two minutes!

Goon snickered and strolled away into the crowd of kids.

"This is Marci's first year at camp. She's from New York City," Lana said.

"It's called the Big Apple," Marci explained.

I knew that.

"You're Georgie, right?"

Georgie nodded. Marci stuck out her hand. Georgie looked at me, then sort of extended his hand. Marci shook it vigorously. She talked fast.

"Lana told me a lot about you, Georgie. You live with your dad, and you want to be a cartoonist or a Navy jet pilot. Me? I live with my mom. She's a pediatrician. That's what I want to be, too. I like cartoons. I don't know much about jet planes."

Then she stopped talking and shaking his hand. Georgie's mouth was hanging open. Marci finally let him loose and said, "Gotta go!" She spun on her heel, pulled Lana with her, and took off, yelling, "Bye, Georgie! Bye-bye!"

* * *

The people who print this book told me it's important for readers to know what the kids in my story look like, but to be honest, right now, while I'm writing this chapter, even though I probably saw Marci a hundred times at camp, I can't remember what color her eyes were . . . or her hair. So now I'm telephoning Lana.

Blah, blah, blah, blah, blah, blah, blah, blah, blah, blah, blah.

Sheesh! Each one of those blahs is a minute. Eleven minutes on the phone! That girl loves to talk. So now I know that Marci's hair is light brown. And her eyes are blue. And she has braces on her teeth with those little colored rubber bands. And she really likes horses. And she has a cat named Blossom. And she didn't lose her first baby tooth until she was almost seven. And . . . And . . . And . . . Sheesh!

* * *

The bus unloading was finally done, and the parents were almost all gone, so Uncle Bud lifted his megaphone and began directing the boys to their side of the Border Line and the girls to the other side, where Aunt Lois was waiting.

The Border Line divides Camp Leeward from Camp Windward. It is made up of yellow dashes painted down the middle of the camp road, yellow rocks in the parking area, a yellow line down the middle of the dining hall, and more yellow rocks from the back of the dining hall to the cliff above the lake.

"The Border Line," Uncle Bud announced over his megaphone, "is uncrossable. The penalty is death or something else . . . my choice!" He says that every year.

Just so you can get an idea of what's where, here's a close-up map I drew of the two camps and Buffle-head Lake. It's not exactly to scale, but pretty good.

If you look at my map, you can see that the can-teen, the computer room, and the nurse's office are

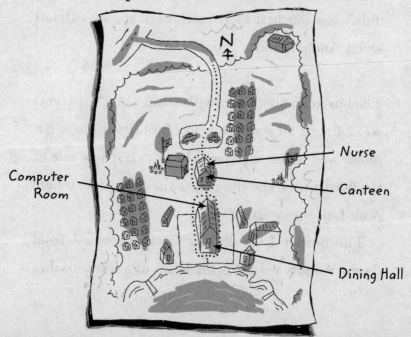

Computer Room

Nurse

Canteen

Dining Hall

special. Because boys and girls share those two facilities, the Border Line goes around them on both sides. They're sort of on neutral ground.

Interesting fact: In the olden days before computers were invented, the computer room was the camp's bakery. You can still see marks on the walls where the bread ovens used to be.

"Seven- and eight-year-old boys," Uncle Bud bellowed through the megaphone, "follow me. Seven- and eight-year-old girls, follow Aunt Lois. The rest of you campers, look at the maps on the bulletin boards. Find the cabins for your age group, grab your gear, and go. Rosters are posted on the cabin doors. If you have quest—"

Georgie, Lenny, Robbie, Evan, and I had already snagged our stuff out of the pile. We didn't need to stick around for the end of Uncle Bud's announcements. And we didn't need to look at the map. We knew where we were going. The eleven-year-olds were in Cabins F and G every year.

Robbie got to the roster at Cabin F first. He ran his finger down the names. "Me, Lenny, and Evan are in here. Cheesie and Georgie must be in G." He pointed at the other eleven-year-old cabin.

I read the paper on the door. Scott Dutcher was the counselor of Cabin F. But Robbie was right. Georgie and I were not on the list. I ran to Cabin G.

"I'm in this one!" shouted Alex Welch from the steps of Cabin G.

I pushed past Alex and looked at the paper on the Cabin G door. "Huh? We're not on this list, either!" I yelled back to Georgie, who was standing with the others, still holding his bags.

I looked around. Uncle Bud's golf cart (we call them campmobiles) was parked in front of Cabin A, the littlest kids' cabin.

"C'mon!" I yelled, and ran uphill. Georgie dropped his bags and trotted after me. He was only halfway there when I got to Cabin A. I almost slammed into Uncle Bud as he came out.

"Georgie isn't . . . He and I aren't . . . We're not in either F or G!"

Uncle Bud stepped back a bit, gave me a calm-down look, and peered at his clipboard. "You're in H."

"H? We're in H? We're with the Big Guys?" Cabin H was for twelve- and thirteen-year-olds. "No, no, no, that's not right! We're Little Guys. We—"

Georgie arrived at my side.

"Georgie was late in applying," Granpa said. "Remember? We were full up. I had to move kids around to make room. I knew you wanted to be together, so I put you both in H. It's no big deal."

I was stunned. No big deal?

"Georgie's bigger and older anyway. And you're a clever kid. You both can handle it. End of story. I'm too busy to argue." He got into the campmobile.

"But, Granpa, we'll barely ever see our camp friends."

"What's done is done." He pressed the pedal, rolled forward a couple of feet, then stopped. "Sorry," he said, then drove off.

Georgie's eyebrows were waggling up and down, and I stood with my mouth hanging open. We had been at Camp Windward for less than an hour, and our summer was already ruined!

Chapter 4

The Toilet on the Wall

We walked back to Cabin F in silence. Robbie, Evan, and Lenny had already gone inside to unpack. Georgie and I picked up our bags and trudged to Cabin H. Sure enough, our names were on the roster tacked to the door. And if I'd looked all the way to the bottom of the alphabetical list, I would have realized why things were going to get ten times worse. We stepped inside . . .

And there was Kevin Welch, glaring at me.

"Get out of our cabin, Runt."

"Cool it," Georgie said. "This is our cabin, too."

"Oh, save me!" Kevin whined in a high voice. "The babies are here to hurt us. We're done for, Ty," he said to the boy next to him.

Ty shot me a super-unfriendly look. Remember Ty? He was the guy who, after I hit Kevin with a spitball, smiled at me malevolently (muh-LEH-voh-lent-lee . . . it means "really evilly" and was also in my first book). I looked around the cabin. Eight bunk beds. There were kids unpacking at every bunk bed except the one way in the back. That top bed had a suitcase on it. The bottom bed had a sticky note on it: *Georgie Sinkoff*. I didn't see a note with my name on it anywhere.

Everyone was looking at us. Although I knew most of these kids from previous years when they were Little Guys like me, I wasn't pals with any of them. This was not good.

Just then a guy walked in. I had never seen him before.

"Good afternoon, boys," he said in a soft voice. "I guess I'm the counselor for Cabin H. My name is Ronald Lindermann."

"You're a newbie," Ty said.

The new guy didn't say anything at first. We all stared at him.

"A newbie?" Lindermann finally said. "Yes. Camp Windward. This is my first summer."

Lindermann had glasses, was only a couple of inches taller than Ty and Kevin, and looked like sports were not his favorite activity. He coughed once, looked around nervously, and continued.

"I'm twenty. I'm a junior at MIT. I'm studying how the brain works."

He paused, but none of us said anything. I knew about MIT (em-eye-tee = Massachusetts Institute of Technology). It's a very famous university for really smart students.

"I'll be your science counselor this summer. Computers. Biology. Pond scum. Things like that."

No one spoke, so Lindermann walked to the bunk above Georgie's, pulled his suitcase down, and began unpacking it into the built-in cabinets near each bed.

Ty whispered to Kevin, "What a nerd."

Kevin turned to me and whispered, "What do you think, Ronald Mack? Makes sense that he's a nerd, right? His name is Ronald, the nerdiest name in the world."

I was trying to think of something to say that would combine Kevin's name with pond scum when two short trumpet blasts came over the camp loud-speakers. That meant dinner. Georgie and I walked to the back of the cabin. He put his gear on the one empty bed. By the time we turned around, all the other kids were out the cabin door.

"What're your names?" Lindermann asked.

"I'm Georgie."

"I'm Ronald," I said. "Like you. But everyone calls me Cheesie."

Lindermann shook our hands.

"Where do I sleep?" I asked.

"Oh, yeah," Lindermann said. "You're the extra kid. Uncle Bud's your grandfather, right?"

I nodded.

"In there." Lindermann pointed at the back wall. Every cabin had a storage closet for extra bed frames and junk. The door had been taken off this one.

I leaned into the closet. It had been cleaned out and set up with a single bed and a small dresser for my clothes and stuff.

"Come on. Let's get to dinner," Lindermann said.

He walked with us up the hill toward the dining hall. But he didn't say much, and neither did we. Three feelings were all mixed up inside me:

1. I was really upset that Georgie and I weren't going to be with our camp friends.
2. I really wanted Dutcher as my counselor.
3. Georgie and I were going to be sleeping in enemy territory.

Our dining hall sits near the edge of a straight-down cliff above Bufflehead Lake.

Don't worry. There's a guardrail. And if you're imagining that it'd be cool to jump into the lake from up there, forget it! It's a thirty-foot drop, the water is only a couple of feet deep, and there are rocks.

One wall of the dining hall is almost all windows, so while you eat there's a terrific view of the lake.

Windwarders and Leewarders enter the dining hall from opposite ends. We eat at the same times and have the same menu, but except for the kitchen window where servers pick up food platters, the boys and girls are entirely separate. In fact, because the kitchen is in the middle, the boys almost can't even see the girls, which is fine with me.

You eat with the guys from your cabin, so when Georgie and I went in, we waved to our camp friends from Cabin F and went to the Cabin H table.

Lindermann pointed at me and Georgie and said, "How about you two serve." Georgie and I moved quickly to the food window (if you're slow, you're last in line). The food at camp is really good, but the first dinner is extra special.

Mookie, the only kitchen worker I actually know, was handling the serving window. "Hey ya, Cheeseman. Welcome back. Here you go." He handed me a platter of fried chicken. Georgie got a bowl of mashed potatoes. I beat him to our table, plunked the plate down, and zipped back to the window just as the kitchen staff was pushing out the salad and the bread. I was hungry and moving fast.

My strategy, because I know that the boy servers and the girl servers come to the window from opposite directions, is always to move into the empty space between the two groups and squeeze forward. This puts me ahead, but also right next to the girls, which usually is not a problem. This time, however, as I got a bowl of green salad and turned to go, there stood Lana Shen. I was trapped.

"Hi, Cheesie. Could you please pass me some bread? I can't reach." I handed her a basket. She gave me a too-big smile.

Mookie grinned from inside the serving window like he knew something I didn't know. I zoomed away.

Interesting fact: Mookie told us that the boys are always messier, but the girls are always louder.

After dinner we were supposed to have a campfire, but it started to rain, so everyone went to the Barn. It's not actually a barn. It's a regular building where we watch movies and do plays and talent shows . . . and where we gather when the weather's bad. The girls have an exact same building on their side of the Border Line, except they call theirs the Ballroom.

When we entered the Barn, it was obvious that no one had expected rain. Chairs weren't set up. Everyone was sitting on the floor.

48

"Look!" Georgie said, pointing to the far wall. "That's weird." The Barn has a stage at one end, with doors on both sides of it. One leads backstage. Georgie was pointing to the other door, which leads to a bathroom.

Attached to the wall right above the bathroom door was Aunt Lois's newest sculpture: an old-fashioned toilet, the kind with a separate tank and pull chain. The bowl was about as high as a basketball hoop. The lid and the seat, painted fire-engine red, were up.

Aunt Lois is an extremely creative person. She is also very strange.

(Later in the summer I found out she attached a similar toilet to the wall of the Camp Leeward Ballroom, except theirs has the toilet seat down.)

Suddenly Kevin and Ty put their arms around Georgie and started pulling him toward the other guys from Cabin H.

"C'mon, Georgie, old pal. Lose that loser," Kevin said, dismissing me with a wave.

Georgie jabbed out both elbows and spun away from them. He looked ready to fight. Ty laughed. Kevin grinned. Anybody could tell they weren't really trying to be friends with Georgie. They just wanted to torture me. Ty and Kevin sauntered (walking like they thought they were super cool) over to where Lindermann and the rest of the Cabin H boys were sitting. At campfires, you have to be with your bunk mates, so we followed, but sat as far away from Kevin and Ty as possible.

Uncle Bud walked onstage. Everyone cheered. The first campfire (even if it has to be inside the Barn with no fire and no way to roast marshmallows or make s'mores) is always a big welcoming. He took the microphone off the stand and started just like always: "Hello, Windwarders!"

"Hello, Uncle Bud!" all the kids and counselors shouted back, not exactly in unison.

Then he began to tell a joke.

He tells this same joke every year, so every

returning camper knows it by heart. And just before he gets to the end, we always interrupt by yelling out the punch line and laughing hysterically. (The joke is on my website, but I warn you, it's only funny if you've heard it a million times.)

"What?" Uncle Bud shouted. "This is the way you treat an old man who's just trying to make you laugh?" He stomped around the stage, shaking the microphone and waving his fist in the air, which made the kids hoot and yell and laugh even louder. Finally he raised both arms, and we all quieted.

"Okay, then. You lose," he said. "No more jokes for you guys!"

All the kids cheered in approval.

Uncle Bud made a mad face, then broke into a big grin, waved his arms like an orchestra conductor, and started singing "Puff, the Magic Dragon." He sings loudly, which somehow makes it easy for everyone to sing along.

About three songs later, my shoe got yanked off.

It was Kevin! He had crawled near me while I wasn't looking. I grabbed at my shoe, but he passed it to Ty, who passed it to kids from another cabin, and in seconds it was all the way on the other side of the room. I lost sight of it.

I don't know how Uncle Bud got it, but when the song ended, he held up my shoe and asked, "Who lost a sneaker?"

I stood up and limped one-shoe-on, one-shoe-off through more than two hundred seated kids. Uncle Bud gave it to me, along with a squinty-evil-eye. I put it on and walked back to my group.

Dutcher took the microphone. "Hey, guys. Want me to tell you about how I bicycled across California?"

Instantly the Barn was filled with "Yes!" and "Sure!" and "Go for it!"

Dutcher waited until we quieted. "Okay. The Tour of California is a very long bike race. It starts in Nevada City, which is actually in California. . . ."

It was a great story, with dangerous zooming down mountains, exhausting sprinting to the finish, and lots of stuff about teamwork. He's especially excellent at describing gory crashes and blood and stuff. I was sitting on the floor, completely relaxed, but as he spoke, I realized I was actually breathing heavily, just like I was one of the guys pedaling. And that was when Kevin snatched my shoe again.

This time it ended up with Dutcher. He stopped in the middle of his story, held it up for everyone to see, and announced over the microphone, "Will the owner of a white and green, somewhat smelly cross-trainer please come to the lost-and-found? Will the owner of . . ."

Everyone laughed.

Then Dutcher looked straight at me. "Cheesie? Is this yours?"

Everyone laughed harder as I limped to get it again.

When the non-campfire campfire ended, the rain was really coming down. Most kids ran to their cabins. Georgie and I walked.

"Kevin and that Ty guy are really bothering me," I said.

"They hate you," Georgie said. "And they hate me, too. Because they know we're best friends."

Even though it was a warm night, the rain gave me shivers. Georgie walked with his head up and his mouth open, catching raindrops on his tongue. We were sopping wet when we reached Cabin H.

After lights-out, I lay in bed thinking. Because my closet was sort of a bump attached to the rest of the cabin, I decided to call it the cove. It had a small, high window that let in the moonlight. I couldn't see anyone because of where my bed was, so I closed my eyes and concentrated on using my hearing.

After a few moments of listening to the rustling of sheets and the squeaking of bedsprings, I realized I could tell whether the noise came from the bunks on the north side of the cabin or the south side. I was musing (MYOOZ-ing is a very good word to use in school . . . means "being deep in thought") about bats and how they use echolocation (even if you don't know that word, you can easily guess what it means) to find their way around in the dark. That was when Kevin—my ears located him on the south side—broke the silence.

"Hey, Lindermann. How about you tell us a ghost story? Something scary."

"I don't know any ghost stories," Lindermann said.

My ears located Lindermann and Georgie on the north side, in the bunk beds closest to the cove. Of course I already knew where everyone's bed was, but it's amazing how accurate your hearing can be when you ignore everything else and use it as your only sense. You should try it. It really works.

"But on my next day off," Lindermann continued, "I could go to a library or bookstore and get a book. How about 'The Legend of Sleepy Hollow'?"

You've probably heard of "The Legend of Sleepy Hollow." It's the story that has the headless horseman in it. If you haven't read it, you absolutely should. It's spooky. It was written by Washington Irving early in the nineteenth century. It's been made into movies, cartoons, plays, and picture books. The original has lots of hard words, but some of the children's versions are really good. And because it's a short story . . . it's short!

"Not out of a book," Ty said. "We want a real story."

If it's from a book, it's not a real story? I thought. Ty is a dope.

The way Ty's voice came into my ears told me that he was in the bunk above Kevin's.

"I think 'Sleepy Hollow' would be great," I said. "It has a headless horseman."

"Shut up," Kevin said.

And that was the way my first night in Cabin H ended.

Chapter 5

Little Big Guy

My second day as a member of Cabin H started out terribly.

Lindermann had already left for flag-raising duty, and while I was in the bathroom doing whatever and brushing my teeth, I heard Kevin yell, "Cheese-Runt wet his bed!"

I stuck my head out the bathroom door. Kevin, Ty, and a couple of other guys were looking into my closet cove, pointing and laughing. I

Just water!

pushed my way through. There was a big wet spot on my bed.

Georgie shoved his way to the front. "It's water! You poured it."

Kevin took a swig from a plastic water bottle. "Nuh-uh. Smell it. I dare you!"

"Don't bother, Georgie," I said.

I was pretty sure no one believed them, but it was still hard not to get embarrassed.

On the way to breakfast, Dutcher snuck up behind me and Georgie and growled like some sort of monster. We jumped, and Lenny shouted, "The Abominable Snowman!"

Dutcher laughed. "Last night I told them about when I was in the Himalaya Mountains and the Yeti"—his voice got mysterious—"came out of the mist. He was big. Bigger than two men. He came closer. I was hanging on to the side of Mount Everest—"

"You never went to Mount Everest!" I said.

"Maybe not," Dutcher said in his normal voice. "But last night's story did."

"Our counselor stinks," Kevin said as we reached

the flagpole. I looked back. There were at least twenty-five kids between us and Lindermann. He couldn't hear. "Our counselor, Ronald . . ."

He made that name sound poisonous.

". . . Lindermann. He says"—Kevin's voice got all whiny—"'I don't know any ghost stories.'"

Dutcher gave Kevin a stern look. "Give the guy a chance, Kevin."

I didn't like agreeing with anything Kevin said, but Ronald Lindermann was definitely not as good a counselor as Scott Dutcher. But then again, I thought, as I put my hand over my heart for the morning pledge, who was?

At breakfast I was still on server patrol, so I walked to the food window. Normally I'd move faster, but I was musing about other names for the Abominable Snowman, like Yeti, Sasquatch, and Bigfoot. (If you know something about Bigfoot, please put it on my website.) I almost bumped into a platter of scrambled eggs that Lana Shen was holding out toward me.

"Take it," she said. "I'm paying you back for helping me last night."

"Thanks," I mumbled, wondering how long she'd been standing there waiting for me. I walked back to the Cabin H table and set it down. I was really hungry. I watched the platter go around the table. When it got back to me, I scooped the last of the eggs onto my plate and noticed both Kevin and Ty were staring at me and grinning.

"Why don't you take a picture? It'll last longer," I said.

I should have been suspicious. I reached for the salt. They were still staring and grinning.

"Stare all you want," I said. "It just makes you look stupid."

I lifted the shaker. Their grins got bigger.

I glared at them, then turned the shaker upside  down over my plate and shook it once. The little silver lid with the holes in it came tumbling off, followed by a land-slide of salt. Kevin and Ty laughed hysterically. I looked down. My eggs were covered with a thick white layer.

There were no more eggs. I ate toast.

After that came morning activity. The other cabins did swimming, sailing, archery, crafts, and every kind of land sport. Cabin H did ballet.

* * *

Hold it! There is *no* ballet at Camp Windward!

I stepped away from my computer for less than a minute to get a snack, and when I returned, someone had changed what Cabin H did to *ballet*. I suspected my dad, who had just gotten into the shower and was singing badly to hide his obvious guilt. So I stuck my head inside the bathroom and asked, but he just sang louder. So I am leaving *ballet* in until he confesses. And just to make sure he confesses, I have stolen his fake foot, which he does not wear in the shower. So if you are reading this, he has not confessed and has either grabbed his foot back from me or is hopping around. I explained why he has a fake foot in my last book. It had to do with a bomb on an aircraft carrier when he was in the Navy.

Okay. Now I am actually several pages further along in the writing of this book, but I am coming back here to insert this explanation: the trickster was *not* my father. It was Goon. She giggled all through dinner and finally admitted it. I should have known. Ballet is one of the things she is actually very good at. I was going to take the whole episode out of this book, but my dad asked me to leave it in. He thinks it's "a good representation of the way our family interacts." Whether I left it in or not, the rules of the Point Battle mean Goon gets points. Here's how I calculated how many. (Look in Appendix A if you want to follow my logic.)

1. Sticking *ballet* into my book was sort of an insult. That meant one point for her because no one else knew about it.
2. But I revealed the insult to Dad. My mistake. That made it two points.
3. When I found out that I had accused the wrong person, that made it embarrassing. Four points.

Since this all happened while I was writing after the summer was over, I can't include these points in the running totals in this book, because the book gets to "The End" before the summer ends.

Get it? The Point Battle is in two places at once.

Wow! This is like time travel.

* * *

What we actually did for morning activity was lacrosse, and I was miserable. I was by far the youngest and way smallest in the twelve- and thirteen-year-old group. Think about it. I was still ten! My birthday was just over a month away. Everybody was better than me in lacrosse, which I had never played before. In fact, this was the first time

I'd ever held a lacrosse stick, which BTW was taller than I was.

Ty and a kid named Jason were team captains. They chose up, and of course I was picked last, with Jason actually saying, "Do I have to take Cheesie?"

Ty couldn't resist. "Nah, you don't. He can go be with the Little Guys. I think they're playing hopscotch somewhere."

It was embarrassing.

I sat on the bench.

"You'll be the first sub," Jason said, trying to be nice.

Yeah, right, I said to myself. I sat on the bench for the rest of the game.

Our second morning activity was computers. Most of the kids played video games (Georgie is a pro!), but I sat at one of the computers and started writing an email about camp to Carlos, my pen pal in Bolivia.

Gumpy, my other grandfather, is a computer science professor at Yale College in Connecticut, and he says the word should be *epal* since pens are irrelevant to computer communication. You probably know where Bolivia is, but just in case, it is a country in South America.

As part of fifth-grade Spanish, Ms. Higgins, my teacher, had connected our class in Gloucester with a fifth-grade class in La Paz, Bolivia's capital city. (Actually, there are two capital cities in Bolivia. The other is Sucre. I don't know why they have two. Maybe Carlos knows.)

Carlos and I email each other almost every week. Here is the first email he ever sent to me:

Hola,

¿Por qué te llamas Cheesie? ¿Es porque te gusta comer mucho queso? Tienes mucha suerte de vivir cerca del mar. Nunca he visto el mar.

Tu amigo de email,
Carlos

Since I was just beginning Spanish and couldn't translate it, I asked my grandmother Meemo to help.

She is excellent in Spanish because after college, she lived for a couple of years in Argentina (which is also in South America). Here's our combined translation of what Carlos wrote:

Hello,

Why is your name Cheesie? Is it because you like to eat a lot of cheese? You are very fortunate to live near the ocean. I have never seen the ocean.

Your email friend,
Carlos

At first I didn't understand about Carlos and the ocean, then I looked on a map and saw that Bolivia is one of only two countries in the Western Hemisphere (North, Central, and South America) that is landlocked—it doesn't touch any ocean. The other is Paraguay.

Anyway, I was almost finished writing a long email (in English!) to Carlos about camp. It would have been the first one he ever got from Maine.

"What're you doing, Runtboy?" Kevin said, sticking his *cabeza fea* (Spanish for "ugly head") between me and the computer screen.

"Stop bothering me," I said.

"You're bothering me by being in my cabin," Kevin said.

"Bug off, Kevin," I said, and then suddenly fell over backward. I looked up. Ty had pulled my chair over.

"Sorry. I didn't know anyone was sitting there," Ty said, then walked away.

I picked up my chair and went back to my email. The screen was blank!

I glared at Kevin.

"Don't look at me!" he said. "You must've hit the delete button when you tipped over."

Carlos did not get an email from Maine. Time ran out.

What happened next was the final straw. We were on the archery range, which is way off in a far corner of the boys' sports fields.

But before I get to that, since Georgie and I were a

few minutes early, we took a long cut (opposite of a short cut) along the Border Line. We were playing Roboto. It's a game we made up, and we pronounce it row-BOAT-oh because we didn't want it to sound exactly like robot. We got the idea from being in the robotics club at Rocky Neck Elementary School. If you're thinking, *Whoa! Nerd alert!* you're wrong. Robotics club was super fun, and it helped me at camp . . . as you'll read later in this book.

This time I was Roboto Boy, and Georgie was the Computer Vision Controller, which we call the CVC. Roboto Boy has to keep his eyes closed—no peeking!—while the CVC gives him directions. The object is for Roboto Boy to walk and move like a robot and get where he's supposed to go without falling or crashing, and especially without opening his eyes.

This might sound like an easy game, but trust me, it's not. It's almost impossible to keep your eyes closed. Something in your brain makes you want to open them. And the longer you keep them shut, the harder it gets. If you want to try this with a friend, the Roboto game, with all the commands and stuff, is on my website.

The CVC (Georgie) was trying to keep my robot feet right next to the Border Line's yellow rocks.

"Straight half. Right mini. Stop. Right mini. Forward full. Don't peek," he said.

Roboto is a game of trust. If the CVC gives you bad commands, you can really bonk yourself. But I trusted my CVC, following instructions like a good Roboto Boy. It had been over a minute since I started Roboto-walking, and I hadn't peeked once!

I heard a bunch of cheeping birds fly above me and head off into Camp Leeward.

"Right half. My voice is going to sound farther away. I'm walking over to get a baseball and throw it back."

I knew we were walking next to the baseball diamond, so that made sense. His voice did start to sound farther away. I kept Roboto-walking with my eyes closed.

"Hi, Cheesie. What're you doing here?"

My eyes popped open. I was standing between two cabins, and there, about six feet away, were Lana Shen, her camp friend Marci, and a couple of other girls. I spun around. Georgie was over fifty feet away, laughing so hard, he had to bend over. He hadn't gone after a baseball. He was still standing next to the Border Line, and had directed me away from the yellow dashes right into Camp Leeward, right toward the girls' cabins, right into No Boys Land!

Without a word to the girls, I ran directly at Georgie as fast as I could and pushed him to the ground. I sat on him and bounced up and down. It didn't bother him a bit. He kept laughing.

"Cheesie? We need to ask you something." Lana and Marci had come over to the Border Line.

"What?" I was mad.

"It's a secret," Lana said. "Come closer."

I climbed off Georgie the Traitor, but stood a few feet away from the girls on my side of the Border Line. "Tell me out loud." I didn't want a girl whispering in my ear.

"Okay. But don't tell anyone."

I nodded. Georgie, still laughing, stood up and came over.

Marci smiled and waved her hand really fast. "Hi, Georgie." Then her face changed, and both girls got really serious.

Lana was almost whispering. "This is a secret. You promise not to tell?"

She looked at me. I didn't do anything. Georgie still had a Roboto-double-cross grin on his face. He nodded. I had no idea what was going to come next, but something told me I wasn't going to like it.

Then Lana turned to Marci, who began talking quietly, but really fast. "Okay. Here's the problem. My brother, Marcus . . . you don't know him. He was supposed to come to camp this summer, but he broke both his legs skateboarding. Really bad. And he's home in bed with his legs all up in the air. You know, in casts with ropes attached to whatever."

"Your brother?" I asked.

"Uh-huh. He's my same age. We're twins . . . fraternal."

(The "frat" part of that word, like in the word *fraternity*, means "brother" in Latin. My dad told me. He's really good with words. But even if the twins are two nonidentical girls, or a boy and a girl like Marci and Marcus, they call them fraternal, like they're brothers. Go figure.)

"Anyway, I phoned him this morning when Lana and I were in the computer room, and he's *really* sad. I mean really sad."

"How'd he break his legs?" Georgie asked.

"Like I told you. Skateboarding," Marci said.

"I know," Georgie said. "But, wow, both legs! What was he doing?"

Georgie and I have skateboards, but neither of us is all that good. We have, however, watched tons of videos of guys doing awesome tricks.

Marci looked confused for a moment. "I don't know. Something dangerous. A double wobbly, I think."

Huh? I looked at Georgie.

Georgie was puzzled, too. "I never heard of a doub——"

"Something like that. I don't know much about skateboarding," she said. "Anyway, I was hoping you guys . . . I mean, Uncle Bud is your grandfather, right?"

I nodded, but I was completely confused.

Marci looked all around—I guess to make sure no one else was listening—which was unnecessary because there was no one even close to us. "Please. I am soooo worried about my brother. He needs me. He needs me to talk to him every day."

"Or text him," Lana said.

"Or text him," Marci repeated. "Every day."

"Does it hurt?" Georgie asked. "His legs, I mean."

Marci didn't answer immediately. She looked up at the sky, then back at Georgie, staring at him so hard he had to turn away.

"It did at first. But now he's just so sad. And I'm really worried."

"Did you see how it happened?" Georgie asked. "The wipeout?"

I don't remember what they said next because I started daydreaming about how I'd write a story about a guy like Marcus if he'd been skateboarding in Sleepy Hollow instead of New York City. I might call it "The Legend of Double Wobbly."

"—and I bet that it's terrible and all that, but what do me and Cheesie have to do with anything?" Georgie asked.

"Well," Lana began, "if you, because he's your grandfather . . ."

She put her hand on my arm, and I jumped. Also, I did not like what I was hearing.

". . . could sneak us into the computer room every day. Like right before dinner?"

They were asking me for help because at camp there are no cell phones or video games. You can bring them on the bus, but once you get to camp, they all go to the computer room, and you can only use them during computer activity periods (about twice a week) or to reply to phone calls that are received on the camp office phone. That keeps kids from texting and chatting and playing video games when they could be having summer camp fun. Some newbies whine and complain, but it's really a great idea. After a couple of days, you don't even miss it. You might not believe me now, but by the time you finish this book, I bet you'll agree.

"Lana says there's no one else at camp who can help. Please . . ." Marci sighed, staring straight at Georgie. "I'm afraid my brother might go crazy."

I took a step backward. "Let's go, Georgie. We've got to get to archery."

"Wait right there," Georgie told the girls as he yanked me about twenty feet away. Then he whispered, "What do you think?"

I shook my head no-way.

"She said he might go crazy."

I shook my head harder. "That's crazy. Marci's crazy. People don't go crazy from broken—"

"How do you know? Remember how upset we were when we thought we weren't coming to camp?"

"Sure, but we didn't go crazy," I said.

"C'mon, Cheesie. Have pity on this Marcus guy. What if you broke both your legs? She's right about the computer room. It's empty right before dinner. You could sneak keys from Uncle Bud. We could sneak the girls in."

"I'm not sneaking anything," I said.

Georgie grabbed both my shoulders and shook me as he spoke. "Think about it (shake). This could be a Cheesie (shake) and Georgie (shake) secret mission (shake)."

Then he leaned real close and whispered like he was telling me the secret words for a magic spell: "And it'll be fun."

My mind was spinning. Here's what I thought:

1. We definitely could do this.

2. We definitely would have fun.

3. We'd definitely be breaking a camp rule.

4. But we'd definitely be doing a good deed.

I looked over at the girls. Both said the same word at the same time: "Please."

"Okay. We'll do it," I said. "We'll hack our way into the computer room with you. Meet us in the dining hall exactly fifteen minutes before dinner. But if you're one second late, the deal's off."

As we hurried to archery, I realized I had agreed to another one of Georgie's Great Ideas.

Chapter 7

The Legend of Double Wobbly

Twilight had come quickly, darkening the steep roadway. I skated over the top of Ichabod Hill and pushed off hard, picking up speed. I could hear dogs in faraway backyards barking and howling at the setting sun. Carving a tight line on the curving road, I shot downhill faster and faster, rapidly approaching the dangerous twists of Double Wobbly. Suddenly a wave of bad feeling came over me. It wasn't fear exactly . . . more of a strange, demented sadness. I could not continue. I dug in, grinding my board to a stop.

Just at that moment the distant dogs went silent, and a nearby rasp of wheels on pavement caught my

ear. I looked uphill. There, concealed in a shadow cast by a dark cloud, a towering figure stood on a glowing skateboard.

My hair rose in terror. Was it the demon of Double Wobbly? Could I outrace this evil? I was fast on my board . . . but was I fast enough?

At that moment the cloud moved off the low sun, and I could see my pursuer clearly.

My heart went cold. The dude on the skateboard had no head!

* * *

In the last chapter, I wondered what a story with a headless skateboarder would be like, so today, while I was sitting in my middle school library waiting for my dad to pick me up (I have a dentist appointment), I reread "The Legend of Sleepy Hollow," then wrote the beginning of my short story.

Mrs. DeWitt, our librarian, suggested the word *demented* (it means "crazy" . . . it's a terrific playground word!) when I got stumped.

Marci had told us her brother had busted his legs doing a double wobbly, but since neither Georgie nor I knew what that was, I turned it from a skateboarding trick into a dangerous place where bad things—like broken legs—happen. And since the main character in "The Legend of Sleepy Hollow" was named Ichabod Crane, I used his name, too.

I don't know if I'll ever finish "The Legend of Double Wobbly," because I have no idea what happens next or why the skateboarder has no head. If you have a good idea, tell me your plan on my website.

Oh, and the reason this is Chapter ? is because it's spooky.

Chapter 6

The Challenge and the Hack

The archery range has nothing but woods directly behind the targets. They built it that way because we use real arrows with metal points. You could really hurt somebody, so the first archery lesson anyone gets is all about safety. Two years ago, I saw a kid aim crazy on purpose and shoot an arrow totally out of sight into the trees. He lost archery privileges for the rest of the summer. They found his arrow stuck in a tree about twenty feet up. It's still there. I've seen it.

I like archery, and I'm pretty good at it. I've gotten better every year since I was nine. (Seven- and eight-year-olds are considered too young for archery.)

We were with another Big Guys cabin at the archery range that morning, and as I expected, I ended up last in line. Most of the guys were not very good. Kevin and Ty each got only one arrow in their hay-bale targets, and neither of those were anywhere close to bull's-eyes.

Georgie and all the other Cabin H bunk mates used large bows. I selected one of the smaller bows meant for Little Guys. They don't shoot as far or as hard, but they're just as accurate, IMO, and much easier to draw back.

"Oh, sweet! That's perfect. A baby bow for the Runt!" Kevin shouted.

"Go ahead and laugh," I said. "You're a lousy shot. I bet at least three of my arrows end up in the target."

Derek, the archery counselor, shouted from the other side of the archery range, "Cut the goofing around and get going! We're almost out of time."

As I nocked my first arrow, I looked toward Georgie (I wanted him to watch me outshoot Ty and Kevin), but he couldn't see me. Ty was standing between us, blocking (on purpose, I figured) his view. I pulled back the bow . . . aimed . . . and just as I let fly, Kevin squirted me in the back of the head with a water pistol he'd hidden in his pocket.

My arrow hit the dirt about ten feet in front of the hay bales.

I turned around angrily, and a second squirt hit me smack in the face.

Everyone laughed.

Derek tried to be stern. "No fooling around when someone's got a bow in his hands." But he was chuckling as he looked at his watch and took my bow. "Time to wrap things up," he said.

As soon as Derek and a couple of kids left to put all the equipment in the archery shed, Kevin squirted me again. I stomped toward him while getting splashed over and over, and exploded. "That's your plan? Being a bully?"

Kevin laughed.

"Face it, Kevin!" I shouted, slapping his water pistol to the side. "What you do is way too easy. Anybody bigger can always pick on someone who's littler!" I'm sure everyone was watching, but I was so mad I couldn't see anything except his stupid face. "Bullying me doesn't win you anything!"

"What're you going to do about it, Runto?" Kevin said, puffing out his chest.

"You're chicken, Kevin! You're a bully and a chicken! You're afraid to face me in a fair fight!" I was so mad I wasn't thinking about what I was saying.

Kevin's smile disappeared. He looked around. All the kids were silent.

"Okay," Kevin finally said. "You want a fair fight? I'll make it as fair as I can. I challenge you to a duel, and you can choose the weapon."

I didn't know what to say. What had I gotten myself into?

"C'mon, Runt," Kevin taunted. "Are *you* chicken? Pick a weapon. You can choose anything."

I was frozen. I couldn't think of a single weapon with which I could beat Kevin. But as I desperately tried to think of something, I suddenly realized that *thinking of something* is what I'm best at! I knew if there was any kind of brain work involved, I'd have a chance to beat him. But I also knew I would have to be tricky. Kevin would never agree to a straight-up quiz contest with questions like "Where do lemurs come from?"

(Lemurs are primates, but not monkeys. I have a page about lemurs—and the answer—on my website.)

Then—I don't know where in my brain ideas like this come from—I had the answer!

"I'll fight you," I announced, looking Kevin straight in the eye. "And since I get to choose the weapon . . ."

I glanced at Georgie. His eyebrows were waggling like they always do when he gets nervous, and he was shaking his head *stop-stop-STOP!* But I couldn't stop. I took a step toward Kevin and spoke loudly. "Since I get to choose the weapon, I pick coolness. The winner will be the kid who does the coolest things at camp—and the guys in our cabin will decide. I accept your challenge, Kevin! You're cool, or you're a fool. I accept your challenge to the Cool Duel!"

"That's stupid," Kevin said, but the rest of the guys were hollering, "Go for it!" and "Yeah!" and stuff like that. Kevin stood alone, fuming mad. Ty came over to him and began whispering. I couldn't hear what he was saying, but Kevin was shaking his head.

Then Jimmy Kelly and Danny Stephens, two Cabin H boys I'd been sort of friendly with last summer when they were still Little Guys, changed the noise into a chant: "Cool Duel! Cool Duel! Cool Duel!"

Kevin gave them a super-mad look, but when lots more boys joined in, Kevin pushed Ty away and said, "Okay, Cheesie. You want a duel? You got it!"

"Shut up, everybody!" Georgie shouted. "I'll be Cheesie's second."

In the olden days, when men fought duels, each man had a trusted assistant—called a second—who would make sure the fight was fair and the weapons were equal.

Interesting fact: In 1804, there was a very famous duel where Aaron Burr, the vice president of the United States—I'm not kidding—shot and killed Alexander Hamilton, the man whose picture is on our ten-dollar bill!

Derek and everyone else began walking back, but Kevin and I (the duelists), helped by Ty and Georgie (our seconds), stayed behind. After a lot of discussion and arguing, we finally agreed on the Cool Duel Rules:

1. The Cool Duel would begin the next morning right after flag raising and last seven days.
2. All Cool Duel activity had to be visible to all the boys in the cabin . . . no secret deals, bribes, or dirty tricks.
3. Only the kids in Cabin H would be in on it. No one else in camp could be told about it, especially counselors and Uncle Bud.

4. We'd have a silent, hand-raising vote every night just before lights-out so we'd know who was winning. The final, deciding vote would come at the end of the seventh day, with each kid voting out loud in alphabetical order. (Kevin insisted on this. His last name is Welch, and he wanted to be last.)

5. The loser would have to stand up during announcements the morning after the final vote and say, "In my opinion, [Kevin or Cheesie—whoever won the vote] is the coolest guy in camp." And then the loser would have to drop to the ground and bow five times to the winner. It would be very embarrassing.

Georgie and I were last to leave the archery range. "This is going to be so awesome. What're you going to do first? You know . . . to get ahead in the Cool Duel."

"I have no idea," I said as we walked toward our cabin. "But after dinner, let's think about—"

Georgie stopped suddenly and grabbed my arm.

"Dinner! The girls! We forgot all about Marci's twin brother's broken legs!"

"We need Uncle Bud's keys!" I shouted, and one microsecond later we were running.

Kids are always running every which way in camp, so even though we sped right past lots of boys, no one paid any attention to us. We were breathing heavily when we got to Uncle Bud's house.

"Shhh." I put a finger to my lips. "Listen . . ."

There was no sound from inside.

Georgie whispered, "Why don't you just knock? If he's not home, great. If he is, just say hello and tell him you want to play with Deeb."

Oh, yeah, I thought. *Duh!*

I knocked. No answer.

I opened the door—which Uncle Bud never locks—and surprise! Deeb was *very happy* to see me. She started jumping, all four legs off the ground, and barking like crazy, so I immediately dropped to my knees and petted her until she quieted down. Then, with Deeb tagging after me, I went over to Uncle Bud's desk and grabbed the extra set of keys hanging on a hook next to his lamp.

I looked at the wall clock. Dinner would start in seventeen minutes. Perfect. I gave Deeb one last head rub, closed her up inside, and met Georgie outside.

On the way to the dining hall, we spotted Uncle Bud walking near the cabins, so we skirted behind the canteen.

(You can *sock* or *belt* someone. I wonder if there are any other clothing words, like *skirt*, that mean to do something unrelated to clothing . . . you know, verbs. I'm going to make a list on my website. You can help me.)

Marci and Lana were waiting outside. I opened the dining hall door and peeked in. It was empty except for one of the kitchen workers putting red and yellow squeeze containers on each table.

"I bet it's hot dogs or hamburgers tonight," Georgie said softly to no one in particular.

"Follow me," I said, "and let me do the talking."

Normally kids come into the computer room through an outside door on the back of the dining hall. It's in plain sight. My plan was to go in unseen by using a locked door that once connected the kitchen to the bakery. (Did you remember that the computer room was a bakery in the old days and that it's attached to the dining hall?) That meant going through the kitchen, which was off-limits to campers.

"Hiya, Mookie!" I called out as the four of us went into the kitchen. "We won't bother you," I said before he could reply. "The camp's got a problem with its data divider. We have to restart the memory multiplier."

He was dropping piles of hot dogs into a giant pot of boiling water. "Can't you go in the other door?" he asked.

"Nope. That's one of the problems. Something to do with Internet interference whenever that door is open."

You can probably guess that what I said was total nonsense. I just strung words together, hoping Mookie didn't know much about computers.

Mookie and the other kitchen workers went back to their tasks while I tried Uncle Bud's keys. After three keys didn't turn, I dropped the ring and had to start over. Then, after about five keys, I lost my place and had to start over again.

"Get it together, man," Mookie said as he walked by us with a tray of buns.

I was a little embarrassed. But there were about a dozen keys on Uncle Bud's ring, and more than half of them were identical except for the zigzag cuts that make each key different. Finally I found the one that worked. I pushed on the door, but it only opened partway because of a computer desk.

"I'll wait in the kitchen," Georgie said.

I gave him a look.

"To stand guard," he whispered.

I nodded, and the girls and I squeezed through the half-open door.

"Okay," I told Marci as I shut the door behind us. "Make it quick!"

I needn't have worried. She was very fast. She ran to the shelves where all the kids' electronic gear was stored, found her cabin's labeled plastic bin, shuffled through a bunch of electronic gadgets, and pulled out the plastic bag with her cell phone. In a few seconds she was tapping her thumbs on the keyboard, texting.

I don't have a cell phone. I'm getting one in September when I start middle school. My sister has one, and she's pretty good at texting, but Marci was super fast. Her thumbs were flying! I walked over to watch, but she turned away.

"It's private," she mumbled.

"Sorry," I replied.

Lana smiled at me.

"Sorry," I repeated.

Moments later Marci announced, "Okay. Done."

She turned off her phone and replaced everything, and we went out the door. We'd been in the room less than four minutes.

Georgie was *not* guarding the door when we reentered the kitchen. He was standing near Mookie, eating a hot dog. I gave him a what's-going-on look, but Mookie was the one who responded.

"Kid was hungry. Wanted one dry. Condiments are out on the tables."

Georgie grinned and opened his mouth to show us. Gross.

I turned to relock the door.

"You gonna need to do this again?" Mookie asked.

"Huh?" I responded.

"How often these computer thingies gonna need jump-starting?"

"Oh, yeah . . . yeah, we might need to come back," I said, recovering quickly. "Maybe tomorrow. It depends."

"Then why don't you leave it unlocked? Won't bother us in here. And next time you won't have to fiddle with all those keys."

"Good idea. Thanks, Mookie."

Georgie held up his half-eaten hot dog. "Thanks, Mookie."

Just as we reached the door leading out of the kitchen, Mookie called out, "Hey, Cheeseman! Think fast!"

I looked back. A chocolate chip cookie was Frisbeeing toward me from all the way on the other side of the kitchen.

If you're wondering if I caught it . . .

Chocolate chip!

Yes!

We reentered the dining hall just as the other campers were streaming in.

"Thanks," Marci said. "I mean for my brother."

"Yeah, okay," I said.

"May I have a bite?" Lana asked, pointing to my cookie.

"Yeah, okay," I said. I broke off a piece for her.

She took it, smiled, and just stood there holding it. Marci was grinning. Georgie was chewing the last of his hot dog. Finally . . .

"We'd better get over on our side of the Border Line now," Lana said.

"Yeah, okay," I said. "Hurry."

Maybe it was the excitement of actually doing the Hack. Maybe it was because the Cool Duel hadn't started yet, so Kevin and Ty didn't do anything at dinner to bother me. Maybe it was Mookie's cookie. Whatever it was, dinner was great. Georgie ate three more hot dogs.

That night, after lights-out, I lay in bed thinking about the Cool Duel. It would start in the morning, and even though I didn't have any idea what I would do, I wasn't the least bit worried.

My last thought before I fell asleep was *Look out, Kevin. Cheesie's coming!*

Chapter 7

The Cool Duel Begins

COOL DUEL DAY ONE

Uncle Bud's wake-up loudspeaker announcement said it was going to be a hot day (shorties on top/shorties on bottom), so I rolled out of bed and sleepily reached for the pile of clothes from yesterday. One benefit of sleeping in the cove is that most of my area was not visible from the rest of the cabin, so I could get away with much more mess than the other kids.

Boom!

In one instant I was fully awake! I couldn't believe what I'd found in the pocket of my shorts.

If you are a careful reader, you probably already know what it was.

Uncle Bud's extra set of keys!

I had completely forgotten to return them.

A few minutes later the trumpet call announced flag raising, and every kid in every cabin streamed out.

"Cover for me," I said privately to Georgie.

He looked at me with a *why* face.

I flashed the keys and then stuck them back in my pocket. He nodded, and his *why* changed to *I got it*.

Uncle Bud would already be at the flagpole, and everyone else would be walking in that direction, so I purposely lagged behind. When no one was looking, I ran toward Uncle Bud's house. I was sprinting across an open area when Deeb, who I guess had been waiting by the flagpole, began running toward me, barking noisily. Lots of heads turned. I was busted.

I don't understand how human brains work . . . especially mine. I didn't consciously think, but I instantly knew exactly what I had to do.

I stopped, changed direction, jumped straight up,

ran a couple of steps back toward the cabins, changed direction again, and repeated. Barking the whole time, Deeb stopped and started each time I did.

I may not know how my own brain works, but I really know how my dog thinks. We'd played this try-to-catch-me game a million times at home.

I zoomed behind Uncle Bud's house, out of sight of the boys watching us, then I reappeared with Deeb close behind. I was trying to convince the watchers that I wasn't a sneaky boy with keys to put back, but an energetic boy playing with his barking dog. Finally, after three now-you-see-me-now-you-don'ts, I secretly ducked into Uncle Bud's house. In less than twenty seconds we were back out, the keys safely on the hook by his desk.

I sprinted to the flagpole and arrived at Georgie's side just as the Pledge of Allegiance began. Deeb's tongue was hanging out. So was mine, and I was breathing too hard to speak until ". . . and justice for all."

At breakfast, after I checked for saltshaker booby traps, I decided to make sure the girls were ready for our next Hack. Jason was our table server, but I got up, popped the last rasher of bacon into my mouth, and grabbed the empty platter. "I'll get some more."

(A rasher is exactly the same as one slice, but my dad told me it's much classier to ask for rashers than for slices.)

I picked up a bacon refill at the serving window and walked to the Border Line. I could see Marci and Lana, but they were several tables away. A girl passed by carrying a refill of French toast.

"Excuse me, could you ask Lana Shen to come over?" I pointed. "She's the girl at that table with the yellow headband and black hair."

The French toast girl didn't change direction. She walked to her table, set down her platter, and yelled, "Hey, Lana! Some guy wants you."

Heads turned, including, to my complete embarrassment, Goon's. Now, you might think this meant points for Goon in the Point Battle. Nope. Even though I was super embarrassed, Goon had nothing to do with it. No points. The score was still 664–661.

When Lana got to the Border Line, I told her another Hack was on for tonight and immediately returned to my table. My cheeks were hot. I'm sure they were bright red.

For the rest of the day, Kevin didn't do anything special, and neither did I. We were like two boxers at the beginning of a fight, moving around the ring, sort of checking each other out, neither landing a punch.

Just before dinner, Lana and Marci met us at the dining hall. This time the Hack was easy. We went into the kitchen, waved to Mookie and the others, and opened the door to the computer room. Marci did her speedy texting thing again, and we were back out in the dining hall in a flash. Georgie tried to mooch food from Mookie, but since the main dish was sloppy joes, you can probably guess that he was turned down.

That night, while Lindermann was in the bathroom (he waits to be last), we held the first Cool Duel vote. At the whispered count of three, each kid held

up one hand. A closed fist would be for Kevin; an open hand for me. Because my bed couldn't be seen by the others, I stood in the cove doorway while I voted.

The total was eleven for Kevin, four for me, with one kid (Sam) not voting. I was off to a terrible start. I sat on my bed, hidden from the other boys, writing down how each kid voted.

I heard Lindermann come out of the bathroom and say, "Lights-out." The cabin went dark.

Sheets rustled. A bed squeaked.

Then Kevin repeated his request from the previous night. "Hey, Lindermann. Tell us a scary story."

"Sorry. Don't know any," Lindermann replied.

Kevin muttered, "Lame."

I lay in my bed with my blanket over my head, looking by flashlight at the list I'd written.

COOL DUEL DAY ONE

ME	KEVIN	
	√	Ty Atkins
	√	Alfie Bickelman
	√	Lloyd Case
	√	Jason Chelsea
	√	Tommy Grace
	√	Noah Keil
√		Jimmy Kelly
√		Cheesie Mack
	√	Zip Matthews
	√	Henry Miranda
		Sam Ramprakash
	√	Ethan Rhee
	√	Clark Rosellini
√		Georgie Sinkoff
√		Danny Stephens
	√	Kevin Welch

I fell asleep thinking, *I've got a lot of work to do.*

COOL DUEL DAY TWO

I woke up thinking the same thing.

While walking to morning activity after break-fast, I asked Jimmy and Danny, "Hey, guys. I've got a question. Why'd you vote for me?"

Danny and Jimmy looked at each other, then Jimmy pointed uphill at Kevin. "He's okay, but I don't want him getting too cocky."

"Do something cool, and you can keep my vote," Danny said.

We had archery again that morning. It was a disaster. Unlike the previous day's archery activity, this time a nine-year-old cabin was at the other targets, and they used all the smaller bows meant for Little Guys. I had to use a Big Guy bow, which was way hard to pull back. I kept flubbing, and when I did get an arrow nocked and aimed, it barely reached the target. Needless to say, my archery performance was not very cool.

I tried all day to come up with something that would win me votes. The Cool Duel was my idea, and thinking was what I was supposed to be good at. My brain wasn't working. Nothing. I felt really stupid.

Luckily I didn't have to come up with anything new for that evening's Hack. We met the girls and went in. Marci worked her phone. We exited. We agreed to do it again the next night. It was a piece of cake.

It really was! Mookie gave each of us a piece of cake. <g>

"Is your brother any better?" I asked Marci.

"I think a little," she said, licking blue icing off her finger.

"When did he break his leg?" Georgie asked, swallowing the last of his cake.

"About . . . I think . . . yeah, about a week before camp started. That's why he's so sad. He was really excited about coming."

"That's why"—Lana took a small step toward me—"we have to keep doing this."

Have you ever had a feeling that something wasn't right, but you didn't know what it was? At that moment I sensed there was something wrong with the Marci/Marcus story, but I just couldn't put my finger on it. (From here on in this book, I'm calling that feeling M&M-itis . . . you know, like tonsillitis or appendicitis.)

All through dinner, M&M-itis was bothering me, but we watched a terrific movie in the Barn that night, and I was so engrossed (which means it held my attention . . . an excellent school writing word), my M&M-itis went away, and I didn't think about it again until . . .

Well, you'll see.

That night Kevin short-sheeted me. That's where someone unhooks your top sheet from the bottom of the bed, folds it up to the top end, and tucks in the sides so when you slide in, your legs hit the fold half-way down and can't go anywhere.

I had never heard of short-sheeting before, but my dad says it happened to him when he was a camper, and it is a very easy way to make someone into the butt of a joke . . . which is what Kevin's short-sheeting did to me. Lindermann and all the guys laughed . . . and I did, too. I had to admit that it was a very cool prank. If you want to try short-sheeting someone, I have instructions and diagrams on my website.

Not surprisingly, the Day Two Cool Duel vote was bad news. Sam still abstained (he didn't

* * *

Mom just called "Wash up for dinner!" So I stopped writing in midsentence to sneak into Goon's room and short-sheet the two beds in there. She and one of her girlfriends are playing outside, and there's going to be a sleepover tonight. I can hardly wait to hear them screech.

ONE HOUR LATER. My mother just stuck her head into my room—I was doing my science homework—and said, "Very funny, Ronald." She'd gone into Goon's room to change the linens and found my booby traps.

"I suggest," she said to me, "you desist from further

acts of aggression." (*Desist* means "No more monkey business, buster.")

No Point Battle increase for me. Darn. But at least Mom smiled. Ha! As soon as she goes downstairs, I am going to sneak into my parents' room and short-sheet their bed!

THREE HOURS LATER. I was in bed reading "Rip van Winkle," another Washington Irving short story (it's about a man who falls asleep and wakes up twenty years later), when I heard my mother scream, *"Ronald!"* and then my father laughed very loudly. Ha!

I am turning off my computer to go to sleep now, but tomorrow after school I will go back to my story's unfinished sentence . . . which I left that way on purpose so I would remember what I was writing about!

* * *

Not surprisingly, the Day Two Cool Duel vote was bad news. Sam still abstained (he didn't vote, saying "I don't like taking sides"), and both Jimmy and Danny switched their votes to Kevin.

COOL DUEL DAY TWO

ME	KEVIN	
	√	Ty Atkins
	√	Alfie Bickelman
	√	Lloyd Case
	√	Jason Chelsea
	√	Tommy Grace
	√	Noah Keil
	√	Jimmy Kelly
√		Cheesie Mack
	√	Zip Matthews
	√	Henry Miranda
		Sam Ramprakash
	√	Ethan Rhee
	√	Clark Rosellini
√		Georgie Sinkoff
	√	Danny Stephens
	√	Kevin Welch

Thirteen for Kevin. Two measly votes for me.

Then came lights-out, and as I lay on my pillow in the cove, I told myself, *Tomorrow is Day Three. You better think up something cool to do. Something cool. Something cool. Something cool.*

I do that kind of thing a lot. My mother says even when you're sleeping, you're still thinking, so I was programming my brain to solve my problem while I slept. Sometimes it works. Not all the time, but if you've got a problem, you should give it a try.

COOL DUEL DAY THREE

This time it worked. When I woke up I had thought of something really cool to do during robotics, which was going to be our morning activity.

I bet you're wondering, *Robotics? At summer camp?*

Yep. This was our first year doing it, and it's great. And best of all, robotics at Camp Windward was actually my idea!

I got the idea last Thanksgiving. My whole family, including my mom's parents, Gumpy and Meemo, was at my house chowing down on the stuffing and stuff (that's my shortcut way to describe our huge Thanksgiving dinner). I can't remember the conversation exactly, but it was something like this.

Granpa (complaining): I got a big problem next summer.

Dad (chewing): What's that, Pop?

Granpa (waving a turkey leg): Crafts. Lots of kids are just plain bored with pottery and painting. And none of them like making take-home gewgaws out of pinecones and twigs. I need to come up with something better.

Gumpy (leaning back in his chair): I'm not surprised, Bud. Today's kids are electronically knowledgeable, twenty-first century all the way. Perhaps they see woodcrafts as irrelevant in their lives.

Granpa (a bit louder): Well, we're not getting more computers. We've got plenty. The kids get all the Internet and email they need.

Me (cheerily): How about building and programming robots?

Goon (snottily): Stupid idea. That would cost millions more than even computers.

I paid no attention to Goon and explained about my robotics club at Rocky Neck Elementary School (I was still in fifth grade then). Our after-school club built little cars that could be programmed to drive over and around obstacles. Gumpy was very interested, but Granpa barely paid attention until I told him my teacher said the equipment wasn't expensive.

(If you want to see what we did in my fifth-grade robotics club, go to the robotics page on my website.)

Since this was the first year for robotics at camp, only a few of my bunk mates knew much about it. So Lindermann divided us into four teams of four each, with the most experienced boys—me, Georgie, Ethan Rhee, and Zip Matthews—as leaders. (Zip's real name is Isaac, but because he is famous for being the slowest guy in every race, he got a zippy nickname.)

The object was to build a robot car and program it to go through a tabletop obstacle course in the shortest time. It would have been total fun if Lindermann hadn't put both Kevin and Ty on my team (also Alfie Bickelman, who is excellent at swimming and sailing, but not much interested in robotics).

"Build it yourself, Nerd Boy," Kevin muttered, pulling a comic book out of his back pocket. Ty sat down next to him.

All the teams got busy building and programming their robot cars. A half hour later, Alfie and I had almost finished putting our team's car together.

"We're missing a wheel," Alfie said.

I looked all around. "We definitely had four when we started," I said.

"Use three," Kevin said without looking up from his comic book. "A tricycle would be perfect for you."

Alfie got on his hands and knees, searching everywhere. No luck. He asked Lindermann for a replacement, but after ten minutes of digging, Lindermann said, "Sorry, guys. I don't have any extras."

Then I noticed the weird smile on Kevin's face.

"Gimme the wheel," I said.

"I don't know what you're talking about," he said.

I knew he was lying.

"Gimme the wheel, Kevin!"

I was mad. So was Alfie.

"Not funny, Kevin. Give it up," Alfie said.

"Oh, hey. What's so uncomfortable?" Kevin said innocently, shifting in his chair. "Oh, look. I'm sitting on a robot nerd-wheel." He tossed it at us, then went back to reading his comic book.

"We don't have much time, Alfie," I said. "But I've got an idea."

Zip's robot car went first and zipped (ha-ha) through the course. Ethan's was fast, too. Georgie's was disqualified because it ignored all the obstacles, never turned, and drove straight off the table at top speed. As it plunged to destruction, Georgie yelled, "Stop, Roboto!"

Alfie and I were last on the course. I hadn't had time to do all the programming, so I knew we wouldn't do the obstacles very well. I didn't care. I had a different plan. I announced, "Our robot car may be slow, but watch closely. It's very cool."

I pressed the start button. It rolled to the first obstacle and stopped.

"Oh, that's very cool," Kevin said sarcastically.

Suddenly, just like I programmed, our car backed

up and began spinning doughnuts (very cool go-in-a-circle moves) with its lights flashing. Then it stopped and spun doughnuts in the other direction.

Everyone cheered!

Except, of course, Kevin and Ty.

As we were leaving to go to our next activity, Georgie whispered to me, "Good job. I bet you get Cool Duel votes tonight from Zip, Ethan, and Alfie."

I hoped he was right.

That evening's Hack went off flawlessly, except for Mookie.

"You know," he said as we entered the kitchen, "I've got a cousin in Farmington who's a flat-out whiz when it comes to computers. I called him up. He says if you guys are having this much trouble every day, he could come over and fix it. No charge."

For a moment, I didn't know what to say . . . and that's why it's great to have a best friend around.

Georgie answered, "Nah. Don't bother him. We can handle it. And Uncle Bud and Aunt Lois are giving us merit badge points. Kind of."

Mookie nodded and went back to his meal prep. "Okay. I get it. You're being good scouts and doing a good deed. Yeah, sure."

What Georgie said was almost a complete and total lie, except we actually were doing a good deed, so maybe that made it okay . . . kind of.

But did Mookie really believe us?

"We're going to have to skip a few days," I said to Marci when she had done her texting thing and all of us were back out in the dining hall.

"Why?" she pleaded.

"I think Mookie's getting suspicious."

"But my brother is so sad . . . ," she said softly.

I looked at her closely. I had that feeling again. My M&M-itis had come back.

"We'll see," I said.

That night, when Lindermann was in the bathroom, I watched Kevin flip his head from side to side as he acted out both sides of a make-fun-of-our-counselor conversation.

Kevin: Hey, Lindermann, how about a scary story?

Whiny Imitation of Lindermann: I don't want to.

Kevin: Why?

WIoL: Because scary stories give kids nightmares.

Kevin: Puh-leeeeze. We love scary stories.

WIoL: I don't know any.

Kevin: Why not?

WIoL: 'Cause I'm a nerd.

Then we had the Cool Duel fist/palm vote, and Georgie's prediction came true. I really zoomed forward! I got votes from Zip, Ethan, and Alfie. And Danny switched back to me. Sam still abstained.

Once the cabin was dark, I ducked under my covers, turned on my flashlight, and wrote down the votes.

COOL DUEL DAY THREE

ME	KEVIN	
	√	Ty Atkins
√		Alfie Bickelman
	√	Lloyd Case
	√	Jason Chelsea
	√	Tommy Grace

ME	KEVIN	
	√	Noah Keil
	√	Jimmy Kelly
√		Cheesie Mack
√		Zip Matthews
	√	Henry Miranda
		Sam Ramprakash
√		Ethan Rhee
	√	Clark Rosellini
√		Georgie Sinkoff
√		Danny Stephens
	√	Kevin Welch

It was 9–6. The tide had turned against Kevin. I was getting close! And since it seemed like Sam wasn't ever going to vote for either of us, if I could switch just two kids, it would be 8–7, and I'd win.

Two more. Two more. Two more. That was what I was saying to myself as I fell asleep.

Chapter 8

Cheesie ↔ Cheesie + Strange Day

COOL DUEL DAY FOUR

The next morning I was the last out of the cabin, and I walked to flag raising with Dutcher and Lindermann.

"Camp photo today. How do I look?" Dutcher asked, strutting like a model in a fashion show.

"Very handsome," I said. "Extremely handsome. Super handsome. More handsome than a—"

He clapped a hand over my mouth, picked me up, and flipped me upside down, holding me by the ankles.

"Are you doing anything for the talent show?" Lindermann asked Dutcher.

"Yep. My usual."

Dutcher does a terrific circus strong-man act. He began lifting me up and down, banging my head on the ground (gently) each time.

Lindermann leaned down toward my head. "I've got a question for you, Cheesie. But if you don't want to answer, no problem. Why does Kevin pick on you?"

I didn't think he had noticed, and I didn't know how to reply. I couldn't tell him about the Cool Duel because of the Rules. Plus, Dutcher was swinging me back and forth by my ankles as we walked toward the flagpole, so talking was really weird. I told him how I hit Kevin with a spitball on the bus.

Lindermann didn't say anything until we were almost to the flagpole and Dutcher flipped me back onto my feet. I was a little dizzy.

"Are you going to be in the talent show?" Lindermann asked me.

"Nah. I don't think so."

The talent show was two days away, while the Cool Duel was still going on. But I wasn't worried

about Kevin's getting votes, because I didn't think he was particularly talented. Unfortunately, neither was I.

Lindermann looked around to make sure no one was listening. "You want to do something with me? Your spitball episode has given me an idea."

He told me about it. He called it JAMPAC.

"I could go into town today to get what we need to build it. You could be the guy who operates it onstage."

I needed two more votes. I needed to do something cool. Working with Lindermann would be risky, because he was definitely not cool, but his JAMPAC sounded totally excellent.

"I'll do it," I said.

When we got to flag raising, I noticed every Cabin H kid except Georgie was holding a huge chocolate bar. Most were still wrapped, but Zip was munching his. None of the kids from any other cabins had any.

"What's with the chocolate?" I asked no one in particular.

"This has nothing to do with the Cool Duel," Kevin replied.

Huh?

"I bought a bunch at the canteen last night. My mom gave me extra money," Kevin said. "I'm just a nice guy who gives out chocolate bars."

"The rules say no bribes," I said.

Kevin smiled a not-friendly smile. "These are gifts to my friends, not bribes."

Who did he think he was kidding? "Totally bogus, Kevin," I said.

"Totally wrong, Cheese-Runt," Kevin said. "It's totally legal. But sorry there's none for you and Stinkoff."

I looked at Georgie. He was biting into a piece he had gotten from Zip, and gave me a chocolaty sheepish grin.

(In addition to *sheepish,* which means "sort of embarrassed," I know *piggish* and *wolfish.* I wonder if there are other animalish words? I am putting a list of real and made-up ones on my website. You can help.)

As we walked from flag raising to breakfast, I realized I needed to come up with something to counteract Kevin's cheatery, absolutely not legal, huge chocolate bar bribes (because that's what they were). But I had no good idea.

Two hours later, my dad came to my rescue all the way from Alaska!

It was a hot morning, and I wasn't thinking about the Cool Duel. I was down at the waterfront, practicing my swimming. In two weeks Camp Windward would compete against other camps in the Bufflehead Lake Swim Meet, and I wanted to race in the individual medley against kids my own age.

In the individual medley you swim four strokes (twenty-five yards each) in the following order:

1. Butterfly—It's the hardest and most tiring stroke.
2. Backstroke—I am very good at this.
3. Breaststroke—My swim counselor says I have good form. I just have to go faster.
4. Freestyle—Because I have excellent breathing

technique, I usually have plenty of energy left to finish.

I was practicing butterfly when a kid onshore yelled that there was a phone call for me in the computer room. I butterflied out of the lake, grabbed my towel, and took off running, flip-flops flying.

I knew the call had to be from my parents in Alaska.

Only one cabin at a time uses the computer room, and that morning—my bad luck—it was Lana and Marci's. Neither girl saw me enter. Marci was head down, texting into her cell phone, and Lana was facing away from me, typing at a computer.

But Goon saw me. Obviously the phone call was for both of us—we'd both been summoned, and she'd gotten there first. I didn't do or say anything. Even so, she pulled her mouth away from her cell phone and snarled, "I'm talking to Mom and Dad now. Sit down, shut up, and wait."

I never like doing anything that Goon commands me to do, but in this case I really had no choice. I plopped down in a chair and shivered.

See if your detective skills can guess why I shivered.

If you said because I was in a wet bathing suit, you're right, but you get only half credit.

Try again. The answer is on page 128.

Then Marci said something to Lana, and both girls giggled. Marci seemed very jovial (JO-vi-al means "happy"). That was a good sign because every time I had seen her previously, she was sad about her brother. But then she noticed me, and her face went from happy to sad in an instant. That seemed weird. My M&M-itis flared up again.

I closed my eyes to think about it, and when I opened them, both girls were standing in front of me, smiling.

"What?" I asked.

They looked at each other, then back at me.

"What?" I said a bit louder.

"Ummm," Lana said, then looked at Marci.

"We were wondering . . . ," Marci said.

"Hey, Runny Nose!" Goon called from across the room.

I ignored her even though my nose was running.

"We were wondering . . . ," Marci repeated.

"About the camp dance tomorrow night . . . ," Lana said.

"You and Georgie . . . ," Marci said.

"We want you both to dance with us," Lana said, then blushed.

Goon, who had walked over just in time to hear Lana, exploded in laughter. "*Dance*? My stupid brother? That's the funniest thing I ever heard!"

And then I blushed . . . big-time. I bet my whole body turned red.

Goon, grinning hideously, held out her cell phone. "Mom wants to talk to you."

I took the phone and said hello, but I was thinking about the Point Battle. Goon would get points, that was for sure, but her insult was absolutely *not* excellent: two points only. The score was 666–661.

I walked outside, which was sort of against camp rules (no cell phones outside the computer room), but I had lots of good excuses:

1. It was way too cold in there for a kid in a
   wet swimsuit.

Answer: Because it's filled with electronics, the computer room is the only place at camp that's air-conditioned. It's really cold in there!

2. I didn't want to talk to Lana and Marci about the dance.

3. Goon was bothering me.

4. I needed privacy to ask my dad for advice about the Cool Duel.

But first I had to deal with Mom. She was being very motherish, asking all sorts of questions about my allergies ("No problem"), brushing my teeth ("No problem"), getting enough rest ("No problem"), and lots more.

"May I talk to Dad?" I think I was a little bit abrupt and might have hurt her feelings. (Sorry, Mom.)

"What's up, Cheesie?" Dad said. He mostly calls me Ronnie when we're face to face.

"I need some advice. Not from you as a dad, but from when you were a camper here. Okay?" Then I told him about the Cool Duel.

(The Cool Duel Rules stated: "No one else in camp could be told about it, especially counselors and Uncle Bud." I was not breaking the Rules. Alaska was definitely not "in camp.")

Dad was very interested. "Your duel ends in four

days, right? So what's going on during that time?"

I told him about the upcoming dance, the annual camp photograph, the talent show, and all the sports and stuff we were scheduled for.

"The talent show, you're going to have to figure out yourself. The dance. Fuhgeddaboudit. But the camp photo," Dad said. "It's today, right? And you're a pretty fast runner?"

He gave me an idea, and I decided to try it.

Right before lunch, the whole camp assembled on a slope in front of the woods for the annual photograph. Every kid gets a copy of the group picture at the end of the summer, and a framed copy goes up on the dining room wall. There are pictures dating back decades to the beginning of the camp. My dad is in lots.

With 240 boys, all the counselors, and Uncle Bud in the picture, the photo is very wide. The photographer uses a special camera. It snaps the people on the left, automatically moves a bit to the right, snaps another picture, moves again, and snaps one more. Later some kind of software turns the three separate photos into one really wide one.

Since I have been a Little Guy every year up to now, and since I am short, I have always stood in the front. This year, as one of the Big Guys, I stood in the very back row, all the way on one side, with Deeb next to me. Georgie stood in the back, too. Except he was all the way on the other side. While everyone was still moving around, I told some of the guys in Cabin H (I definitely did not tell Kevin and Ty) that I was planning to do something very cool.

Once the photographer got everyone positioned, he said, "Say cheese." (When I was with the Little Guys in previous years, Robbie, Evan, Lenny, and the rest of the guys in my cabin would always yell "Cheesie!")

Then the camera clicked, and here's what I did:

1. I waited a split second, smiling Cheesily.

2. Then I turned and sprinted behind everyone as fast as I could. No one interfered because they were all facing the camera.

3. A split second before the camera snapped the third photo, I hopped into the back row on the other side right next to Georgie with an even Cheesier smile.

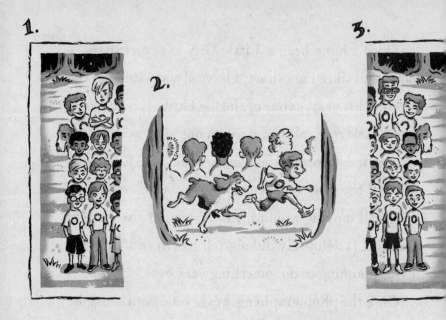

It worked! You can see for yourself. I am my own identical twin, in the photo twice!

Uncle Bud: I bet you didn't realize there's a Cheesie ⟷ Cheesie photo until you read this book.

And if you look closely, you can see Deeb on both sides, too. She's even faster than I am.

On the way to lunch, lots of kids were talking about what I'd done, and I got plenty of back pats and high fives.

As we entered the dining hall, Noah Keil, a Cabin H guy who had never really spoken to me before, put his arm on my shoulder and said, "Wicked cool stunt, Cheesie, but you might come out all blurry."

"Maybe." I grinned.

"How'd you know it would work?" Jimmy Kelly asked.

"My dad was a camper here." I gestured toward the wall covered with old annual photos. "He gave me the idea."

"Wicked cool," Noah repeated.

He and Jimmy walked off to the Cabin H table, but I stood, staring at the old photos. I had a hunch, so I looked closely. It took me a while, but finally I saw what I suspected. In the picture from twenty-four years ago, one kid was in there twice. It was my very cool dad!

I felt confident about my progress in the Cool Duel until our afternoon activity: volleyball. Normally this would be fun because my speed and agility mostly make up for my shortness, but this time? No way. Here's why:

1. We were playing against the other twelve-
   year-old cabin. They were very good, and

the match was very competitive, so I mostly sat on the bench.

2. Kevin is really, really excellent at volleyball.

3. He has a killer serve.

4. He was the star.

5. We won.

Kevin was awesome. There was one volley where he dove and nicked the ball with two fingers just high enough for Clark to set it up for Kevin to come back and spike it. Even the other team commented on that point. And after the match, everyone (even Georgie) cheered for him. Even (I admit it) me.

I had expected to do better in that night's Cool Duel vote, but Kevin's awesomazing volleyball performance more than neutralized my double-photo run. Here's the tally:

COOL DUEL DAY FOUR

ME	KEVIN	
	√	Ty Atkins
	√	Alfie Bickelman
	√	Lloyd Case

ME	KEVIN	
	√	Jason Chelsea
	√	Tommy Grace
	√	Noah Keil
	√	Jimmy Kelly
√		Cheesie Mack
	√	Zip Matthews
	√	Henry Miranda
		Sam Ramprakash
√		Ethan Rhee
	√	Clark Rosellini
√		Georgie Sinkoff
	√	Danny Stephens
	√	Kevin Welch

Twelve to three.

Really bad. Stinking bad. Dead skunk on the high-way, super-smelly bad. I'd lost almost everything I'd gained . . . and there were only three days to go.

COOL DUEL DAY FIVE

At breakfast the next morning, Aunt Lois announced, "Today is Strange Day." The dining room got very noisy in anticipation. "The rule for this year's Strange Day, which will last until dinner is over, is"—she paused and put the palm of her hand on top of her purple-and-orange-striped hair—"you may talk only if one hand is flat on the top of your head."

Immediately kids began chattering, hands on heads. It was fun eating breakfast that way, although it made it hard to cut anything and talk at the same time.

Try it with your family or friends for a few hours. It's easy to mess up, especially if you are thinking about other things. Like when, as we were leaving breakfast, Marci and Lana asked us for another Hack.

"I don't know," I said. "Mookie may—"

"Your hand's not on your head," Lana said with her hand on her head.

I put my hand on my head, but before I could continue, Marci interrupted, her hand on her head.

"But I absolutely have to wash my hair before

dinner or it won't be dry, so can we do the Hack after the dance?"

The dance! My hands instinctively went out in front of me in a stop-it gesture, and I blurted, "Whoa!"

"Your hand's not on your head," Lana said again, grinning.

"Everyone has to be strange on Strange Day," Marci added, grinning even more. Both girls had hands on their heads. Georgie, too.

"Come on!" I was exasperated (great word . . . means "fed up"). Suddenly Georgie reached out and put his other hand on my head.

"This is *not* breaking the Strange Day rule," Georgie explained. "Aunt Lois did not say it had to be your own hand."

Now I could speak, but I said nothing. I couldn't think straight. Here's why:

1. I did not know how to dance.

2. I did not want to dance.

3. If I tried to dance, I would look so completely uncool that when it came time for the Cool

Duel vote, everybody—even me—would
vote for Kevin!

4. I did not want to do a Hack that night.
Something about those girls was still
bothering me. M&M-itis!

5. Georgie was pressing down way too hard on
my head.

I was in an impossible situation. So I did something
I'm not proud of.

I'd rather not write about it, but I promised myself
(and you, I guess) that I'd tell the truth in this book.

What I did was uncool to the max. Luckily none of
my cabin mates were watching.

I ran away.

Chapter 9

Dance Double Cross

I was sitting on a log by the waterfront staring at Aunt Lois's gnome statue in the lifeguard station when Georgie caught up with me.

He put his hand on his head. "I knew you'd be here."

I didn't feel like talking. I could hear a loon on the lake. Loons are like ducks. They have a very spooky, mournful call. I put their sound on my website. If you listen to it, you'll understand how I felt.

After a long time, Georgie put his other hand on my head. "We've been way too friendly with those girls."

"Uh-huh." I felt like a complete dope.

We sat silently. He dropped his hands. I continued

to stare at the gnome while forcing my mind to focus on only one thing: How to Avoid Dancing.

Focus. Focus. Focus.

It didn't work. Here's what went through my mind:

1. I don't want to dance.
2. That gnome is staring back at me.
3. So what? That gnome is not real.
4. Yeah, but what if gnomes were real?
5. Wouldn't it be weird if a real gnome walked out of the woods right now?
6. Even better, what if an alien walked out of the woods right now?

I don't know why my brain does things like this, but suddenly all I could think about was extraterrestrial life. I put my hand on my head.

"Hey, Georgie. Have you ever wondered why almost every alien in the movies or TV, except for insect aliens, which of course look like insects . . . why every alien always has two legs, two arms, and a head?"

Georgie looked at me strangely, kind of like I was an alien, I guess.

I continued, "Well, I think real aliens could come in almost any shape. I bet it's because movie and TV aliens have human actors inside their costumes, and it would be really hard to act if you had to operate five legs like a starfish or if you had your eyes on the end of long, wiggly stalks."

"Or"—Georgie put his hand on his head—"if you had to talk with a hand on your— Oh! Oh!" Suddenly he stood and started fidgeting like his words couldn't wait to come out. "I've got it!" Georgie took his hand off his head. "There's no one watching. Can we just talk normally?"

I looked around and put my hand down, too. "Yeah, I guess."

"Okay. We have to go to the dance tonight. All Big Guys have to. No way out of that. But look. It'll be crowded. We'll move around. Avoid them. If they can't catch us, they can't talk to us. No talking . . . no dancing."

I instantly brightened. "Georgie, that is absolutely another of your Great Ideas."

He nodded. "I call it the Spy-and-Shift Strategy."

"It's perfect. But we have to be super sneaky. If the guys realize what we're doing, it'll be total stink for me in the Cool Duel."

We high-fived and didn't worry about the dance or the Cool Duel for the rest of the day. Here's why:

1. Our morning activity was sailing, so other than when Kevin and Ty's boat tried (unsuccessfully) to ram the ship commanded by Admiral Sink (I was Georgie's crew), I managed to stay out of Kevin's way.

2. At lunch the girls wanted to talk to us (standing at the Border Line with hands on their heads), but we ignored them.

3. In the afternoon, Lindermann split our cabin into two groups, and using compasses and maps, one team went east (mine and Georgie's) and the other went west (Kevin and Ty's). Each group hiked through the woods past lots of checkpoints and raced to see who'd get back to camp first. It took hours, and the only time we saw each other was when the two groups passed about

halfway around and Kevin tried to trip
me. (I saw it coming and jumped out of the
way.) Our team won by nine minutes.
Here's my map:

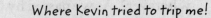
Where Kevin tried to trip me!

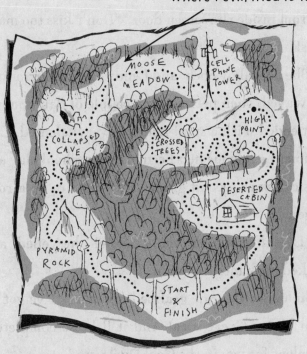

I figured neither Kevin nor I had gained or lost
Cool Duel votes all day.

An hour after dinner, wearing clean shirts
(Lindermann insisted), Georgie and I headed for the

Barn with all the Big Guys. Little Guys are not invited to dances, so we knew from past experience they'd be having a game night in their cabins (you know, Risk, Uno, Monopoly, Sorry!, card games . . . whatever). As we passed by Cabin F, a voice called to us from inside the screen door: "Don't kiss too many girls!"

The door flew open, and Lenny came out grinning. He waved, then performed a couple of dance moves that ended with a spin! Lenny is very talented. Last summer he told me he's been in every school play and musical since second grade. He wants to be a rock singer.

"Lay that one on 'em, Cheesie!" he yelled, and ducked back into his cabin.

Suddenly Georgie grabbed my arm. "I've got an even better Great Idea! And it'll be so completely excellent for you in the Cool Duel vote."

In the last of the sunlight slanting through the trees, I could see a devilish gleam in his eyes.

"If my Spy-and-Shift Strategy doesn't work"—he paused—"we dance with them."

I couldn't believe my ears. "That is definitely not a Great Idea."

"You're wrong. It's the Dance Double Cross. And here's what makes it great."

I listened . . . asked a couple of questions . . . and finally agreed. "It's so stupid, it just might work."

We ran into Cabin F. Lenny was playing Monopoly on a bed with Robbie and Evan.

"Lenny! We need a dance lesson. Right now!"

Every kid in Cabin F stopped what he was doing and watched.

A few minutes later we joined the rest of the boys in the Barn. The girls hadn't arrived yet, so we scoped out the room and talked about how we'd do the Spy-and-Shift Strategy. Then all the girls arrived and everything changed:

1. The sound in the room instantly went from chatter to CHATTER.

2. Maybe the boys had gotten cleaned up a little, but the girls looked like they were at some high-class wedding. They were in dresses, fancy hairdos, and tons of makeup.

3. Someone started the music.

4. Someone dimmed the lights.

5. Someone plugged in a light machine that sent rotating colored lights swirling all around the room. It was actually kind of neat.

* * *

Side note: My mother just came into my room with clothes still warm from the dryer for me to fold and put away. She plopped the load on my bed without saying a word because when I'm writing or doing my homework she doesn't interrupt. But as she was leaving she glanced at what I was writing and asked why Lana and Marci were permitted to go to the dance since they were the same age as me and Georgie, and if we had been Little Guys like we were supposed to be, we wouldn't have gone . . . so why did they?

Good question!

I never thought about that during the summer. Did you think of it while you were reading?

So right now as I am writing this I paused . . .

. . . and went downstairs and asked Granpa. He is watching the World Series and is very cranky that the Red Sox aren't in it. He says that girls mature earlier than boys, so Aunt Lois lets the eleven-year-old girls decide for themselves if they want to go.

I guess that sort of makes sense if you believe that stuff about maturity.

* * *

Even with more than two hundred girls and boys milling around, I spotted Lana and Marci across the room. They hadn't seen us yet, so I grabbed Georgie and ducked behind one of the big speakers. Because Georgie is so tall, I pulled hard and bent him over.

It actually was a pretty lame hiding place, because less than a minute later I heard, "Call an exterminator, Kevin. I found some cockroaches."

We were busted. It was Goon, holding hands with Kevin and grinning big-time. She must have been watching us.

"Dork! Dork! Dork!" Kevin said over and over. He sounded like a sick penguin.

Music was playing loudly, but I didn't really hear it. Lights were flashing and whirling, but I didn't really see them. I knew that her cockroach insult had just hit me for two Point Battle points, and in a battle a trained warrior doesn't just accept an attack and die. He fights back! And that was what I did.

I honestly don't know how I thought of my counter-attack. It just happened. I jumped out from behind the speaker and pointed at the dark makeup gooped all around Goon's eyes.

"Hey! I didn't know this was a costume party. Great job, Junie! You look exactly like a raccoon."

Goon turned bright red, smacked my pointy finger, and stomped away, dragging Kevin behind her.

Mine was a *really excellent* insult. Double points. Two for her. But *four* for me. Ha!

The Point Battle score was 668–665. I was just three points behind.

I was snapped out of my Cheesie vs. Goon thoughts by Georgie's elbowing me in the ribs. He pointed toward the dance floor. Lana and Marci were dancing with each other.

"They're pretty good," Georgie said.

They actually were. I looked at all the other dancers. They were mostly girls and a few older boys.

We watched for a while, making sure to keep tabs on Lana and Marci.

Then Goon started dancing with Kevin. Like I said earlier in this book, Goon is very good at ballet. But I had never seen her at a boy-girl dance, so I was amazed at how excellent she was. Kevin was just sort of standing there, waving his arms and moving his feet a little. I wanted him to be a terrible dancer, but actually he wasn't.

"Your sister is really good," Georgie said.

I looked at the kids standing near Goon and Kevin. Most of my cabin mates were watching them. Even though Kevin wasn't doing much, Goon was so terrific, she made him look very cool.

"Uh-huh. Major bonus for Kevin in the Cool Duel vote," I replied.

Then I saw Dutcher. He was doing these robot moves that were ninety-nine times better than anything Georgie or I have ever done in our Roboto game.

That got me thinking about why I don't like dancing. Here's what I came up with:

1. If you're not good at dancing, you look
   stupid.
2. People stare at you when you're dancing,
   and you get self-conscious.
3. Dancing seems like a girl thing.

But there was Dutcher—a guy I really admire—
out in front of everyone . . . dancing. And that got me
outthinking myself:

1. If you're not good at dribbling a soccer ball
   or hitting a baseball, you look stupid . . .
   but that never bothered me when I was just
   learning to play.
2. People stare at you when you're doing
   sports . . . and even if I'm not very good—
   like in tennis—I don't get self-conscious.
3. Cooking seemed like a girl thing before
   Meemo told me that lots of the world's most
   famous chefs are men.

It was very confusing, but I didn't have time to
think about it because when the song ended, we could
tell that Lana and Marci were looking around for us,
so we used Georgie's Spy-and-Shift Strategy. We

spied on their movements and constantly shifted to the exact opposite side of the room, making sure to stay behind kids or other things that could hide us. That worked for about thirty minutes. Then some counselors brought out refreshments (punch and a huge pile of really good cookies), and we sort of got distracted. A song ended and suddenly the two girls were standing right next to us.

"Hi, Georgie," Marci said.

"Hi, Cheesie," Lana said.

I looked at Georgie. His mouth was stuffed with cookies. The girls were staring at us. I had no idea what to say, but I was holding a cookie in my hand, so I blurted, "These are excellent cookies," and stuck the whole thing in my mouth. The music started again.

Marci picked up a cookie, took a small bite, smiled, spun back and forth on one foot, and shouted above the music, "Lana and I were wondering if—"

I interrupted her by suddenly bowing from the waist. That was our preplanned signal to switch Great Ideas: goodbye, Spy-and-Shift; hello, Dance

Double Cross. Georgie immediately copied my bow.

"May I have the honor of dancing with you?" I said to Lana. I had seen this in the movies.

"And may I have the honor of dancing with you?" Georgie said to Marci.

The girls were very surprised and maybe a little embarrassed. They looked at each other, then nodded.

If you're wondering how much Georgie and I could have learned about dancing in one three-minute session from Lenny, keep reading!

We walked to the center of the dance floor.

Marci and Lana followed.

Once the girls started dancing, we joined in, moving our arms a little, shaking our tails a little, and shuffling our feet just enough to show that we weren't frozen statues. We were not very good. Actually, we were really terrible.

Out of the corner of my eye, I saw Goon stop dancing and stare.

After about ten seconds of our boring dancing, I spun around on one foot the way Lenny had done on the Cabin F porch. Except Lenny didn't stumble over his own feet like I did! It didn't matter, though. The spin was my signal to Georgie.

We looked at each other and counted loudly in time to the music: "ONE! TWO! THREE! FOUR!"

That was how we began the most energetic, outstandingly awful sequence of dance moves ever seen in Maine, the United States, and the whole Western Hemisphere.

We jumped,

flapped our elbows like demented chickens,

fell to the floor and made snow angels,

popped up and hopped in a circle,

kicked left and right while saluting, bent over and waved to the girls, straightened up and did jumping jacks, and ran in place with our fingers in our ears.

And then we did it all over again.

The girls stopped moving. They looked stunned. The other dancers moved away from us, clearing out an area in the middle of the floor. Even though it was exhausting, we never stopped doing the Dance Double Cross.

Finally, as the song neared the end, I grabbed Georgie's hand, and we began running full speed in a tight circle. Then, on the last note, we let go and fell to the floor, our speed making us crash and tumble away from each other and slide across the dance floor.

I looked up at Lana and Marci. They were in shock.

Goon kicked my shoe to get my attention, stuck her finger down her throat, and pretend-puked on my head.

"Dork," Kevin penguined at us. "Dork. Dork."

People were pointing, applauding, screaming, and laughing at us. But so what? Georgie's Great Idea had totally worked! We were so terrible, I was sure Lana and Marci would *never* want to dance with us again!

I was right. The two girls had walked away. And for the rest of the evening they totally avoided us. Georgie and I listened to the music, had more refreshments, and laughed with lots of other guys until the dance was over. We had a terrific time.

But when it came time for the Cool Duel vote, my good mood disappeared. Georgie had predicted the Dance Double Cross would get me lots of votes, but I gained only one. Goon's dancing had made Kevin look really good. Ethan said my dancing wasn't cool. Zip said it was. Danny agreed with Zip and switched back to me. Sam abstained. Everyone else stayed the same. It was 11–4 again.

COOL DUEL DAY FIVE

ME	KEVIN	
	√	Ty Atkins
	√	Alfie Bickelman
	√	Lloyd Case
	√	Jason Chelsea
	√	Tommy Grace
	√	Noah Keil
	√	Jimmy Kelly
√		Cheesie Mack
√		Zip Matthews
	√	Henry Miranda
		Sam Ramprakash
	√	Ethan Rhee
	√	Clark Rosellini
√		Georgie Sinkoff
√		Danny Stephens
	√	Kevin Welch

Only two days left. The next day was the talent
show. I needed to do something big, and Lindermann's
JAMPAC seemed to be the only thing I had going.

Chapter 10

JAMPAC

Before I go on with this story, I want to explain something about the Dance Double Cross:

1. Even though our colossally stupid dancing was ridiculous, neither Georgie nor I were the least bit embarrassed. I guess you can only be embarrassed if you agree that what you're doing is embarrassing.

2. So even though Goon's dancing was excellent and ours was dumb and people laughed at us, because Goon had nothing to do with our Dance Double Cross, the Point Battle was not involved. Zero points.

3. A girl (her name was Naomi, but who cares,

because she will never be mentioned in my books again) told us that we had completely ruined the dance.

4. Dutcher (whose opinion is way more important than Naomi's) complimented Georgie and me. "You guys have a lot of courage. If you work on your moves a little before the next dance, you'll be awesome." I hadn't thought of that. There'd be another boy-girl dance in a few weeks in the Ballroom.

COOL DUEL DAY SIX

With Kevin so far ahead in the voting, he changed his behavior and played it safe. He was strangely nice to me all day, especially when our cabin mates were near. During morning activity, he even chose me to be on his soccer team. (We won 5–2, and I scored one goal.)

Lana and Marci made no attempt to talk to me or Georgie at breakfast or lunch.

In the afternoon, Lindermann pulled me away from our cabin's activity (swimming and sailing) and took me into the Barn, where we worked in secret on our talent show act.

"We'll hide it behind the curtain, and the JAMPAC will be the final act in the talent show," Lindermann told me. He showed me what to do, and I practiced, but I just couldn't get it right.

"I think you're too small," Lindermann said.

"No problem. I'll get Georgie to help," I said.

At dinner, I was surprised to see Lana motioning to me from the Border Line. I tried to pretend I didn't see her, but it was pretty obvious I did, so finally I got up and walked over.

"Hi," she said.

"Hi," I said.

She looked very uncomfortable.

"Um, Cheesie . . . I need to tell you . . ." Then she turned suddenly and moved quickly back to her table. I started to leave.

"Wait!" Marci called out.

I stopped. Marci came over to the Border Line.

"I need to get in touch with my brother. He's unbelievably sad. It's crucial."

"I don't know. I mean, there's the talent show—"

"I know that. Ours is tonight, too. So we'll have to do the next Hack tomorrow before dinner, okay? Promise me. Okay?"

"It's risky," I said, "but . . . all right."

"Okay." Marci took a deep breath, then pointed a finger right at me. "You were really mean to embarrass Lana at the dance last night. She was crying and everything. What you did was just awful."

I didn't know what to say. It kind of was Lana's own fault. If she hadn't asked me to dance . . .

Marci walked away, and I went back and finished my meal. I didn't want to feel bad . . . but I did.

All the boys gathered in the Barn after dinner for the talent show. Everyone was yelling and screaming when Dutcher, as usual, started the show. He came out costumed like a circus strong man, followed by a bunch of seven-year-olds all dressed in camp shorts and T-shirts. Dutcher strutted around flexing and posing, then stood facing the audience, legs spread and arms akimbo.

(*Akimbo* is a word my dad taught me. It means "with hands on hips, elbows pointed out." He told me that it comes from an old English word for a bent archery bow, which is exactly what your arms look like when you stand like that. But the word looks to me like it should be African. I'm not saying that I actually know any African words, but lots of African languages have terrific names, like Swahili, Ndebele, and Wolof . . . and that's what *akimbo* looks like to me. I'm going to stand like that right now. . . . Okay, I did! You should try it. With arms akimbo and your feet spread a bit, you'll look strong . . . like Dutcher.)

Dutcher interlaced his fingers and placed them palms down on the top of his head. One by one the little kids began climbing up like he was a human jungle gym. The first sat with his legs around Dutcher's neck. The second and third perched on each of his biceps. Number four hung from his neck like a necklace. Five and six straddled his hips, hanging on to each other's hands front and back. Then,

with Dutcher struggling to keep his balance, another counselor came out and lifted the littlest kid up over all the others and plunked him onto Dutcher's head. Seven kids!

The average seven-year-old weighs 51 pounds—I looked it up online—so that's 357 pounds, more than one-sixth of a ton!

Next came three Big Guys who were excellent musicians. They did piano, guitar, and violin solos, and then played a piece together. Those guys must really practice.

Then Kevin appeared! I had no idea he was going to be in the talent show. He didn't say a word. He began juggling three baseballs, and everyone applauded. He added a fourth baseball, and everyone cheered. He was really good. He stopped, bowed, and rolled a cart onto the stage. On it were a watermelon, a dinner plate, and a gigantic kitchen knife. He picked them up one at a time and made motions to show how he was going to juggle all three. The audience began screaming with anticipation. Then he surprised everyone by putting the watermelon on the plate, cutting off a slice, and taking a big bite. He bowed and left the stage to huge applause.

Bad news for me. I had underestimated Kevin. It was a very cool act.

(I tried to teach myself how to juggle last winter, but I broke a lamp, so Mom made me go outside, but it was too cold, so I quit. In Massachusetts, I think juggling is a summer activity.)

After a couple more acts I won't describe because they were worse than terrible, it was Uncle Bud's turn. He always does the same talent show act (just like he always tells the same joke at the first campfire). He walked to the center of the stage carrying a phone book. With great dignity he opened it and began reading names and addresses with lots of emotion and long pauses, as if he were reciting poetry.

If you want to know what Uncle Bud's act was like, stand up right now and read the following out loud . . . with great dignity, lots of emotion, and occasional long pauses.

Marrowfield, Margaret J, 124 Winterhaven Circle
Marrowfield, Matthew, 55 Flagstone Road

Marshak, Norbert B, 616 E Eagle Park Drive

Marshmallow, Benjamin, No Address Listed

The audience let him get through four or five . . . then, because we always do it, everyone booed. He pretended to be hugely offended and walked offstage to gigantic applause.

The applause didn't stop, because next up was the Great Georgio. If you read my first book, you know that Georgie is an excellent magician. This is his third year doing magic at camp, and all the kids (except newbies, of course) really look forward to his tricks.

Georgie came onstage wearing his magician's hat and a bow tie. Waving his wand around, he made a bouquet of fake flowers appear and disappear. Next was an excellent now-you-see-it-now-you-don't with a large coin, and then a bunch of sleight-of-hand card tricks. By the time he did his final trick, which included pouring water and sugar into his hat and putting it on his head (where did the water and sugar go?), the audience was amazed. Georgie is super good!

Finally it was time for JAMPAC.

I came out from behind the curtain wearing a white "lab coat" (a dress shirt Lindermann borrowed from a tall counselor), made a deep bow, and spoke very loudly and with great authority.

"Campers and counselors of Camp Windward! Allow me to introduce myself. I am the world-famous mad scientist, Dr. Frank N. Cheez, and this"—I pointed offstage—"is my trusty assistant, Ee-Gorg the Insane."

Georgie (who had made a super-fast costume change) shambled out. He was wearing messy, torn clothing, and his face was smudged. He stomped around the stage, making evil and demented (I love that word!) faces at the audience. The campers cheered and booed.

When the crowd quieted down, I continued. "Today is a day we will long remember." I tried to sound like a governor or senator giving a speech. "Today I give you JAMPAC, a secret weapon so powerful, so awesome, so amazing that once word spreads, every camp in this state and throughout the world will know that Windward is the best."

There were huge cheers.

I gave a signal, and the curtains opened to reveal a large blue tarp with something under it. The cheers turned to oooohs.

I pointed into the audience. "With the help of my distinguished fellow scientist, Professor Ronald Lindermann of the Massachusetts Institute of Technology . . . Would you please stand and take a bow, Professor?"

Lindermann stood, bowed low, and sat back down.

"With the help of Professor Lindermann, and at a cost too infinitesimal to calculate"—*in-fih-neh-TEH-sih-mull* actually means "infinitely tiny" . . . I figured most of the kids would think it meant "infinitely large"—"this awesome device was assembled in secret this morning on this very stage. Campers and counselors, I give you JAMPAC! The Jumping Air Mattress Paper Ammo Cannon!"

With everybody screaming and cheering, Georgie pulled off the tarp. Under it was a contraption of white plastic tubing, hoses, and a pumped-up air mattress. I grabbed a roll of toilet paper and held it high.

"First I prepare the projectile." I tore off about twenty squares, wadded them up, and dunked my hand into a bucket of water.

From the audience Lenny yelled, "Wind-WHOOP! Wind-WHOOP!" and others joined in. I held up my dripping hand. The Wind-WHOOPs continued in a whisper.

"Next I mold this dangerous material into a ball . . . squeeze out the excess moisture . . . and insert the ball into the barrel using this special device"—I picked up a toilet plunger and pushed the wad down the tube with the stick end—"to position the projectile at the bottom of the barrel."

The audience quieted in anticipation.

"Ee-Gorg, please take your position."

Georgie grunted, "Yes, master," and shambled over to the far side of the stage.

"Now I set the Power Escape Valve to the ready position." I flipped a lever in the pipe assembly.

"Then"—I pointed at Aunt Lois's toilet-on-the-wall sculpture—"I aim."

The crowd looked where I was pointing and went crazy!

I leaned over, examined the tubing, and pretended to move it slightly (we had already aimed and tested it). I raised both my arms, and the audience immediately went silent.

"Fire!"

Ee-Gorg ran toward the JAMPAC, leaped high, and slammed both feet down onto the air mattress. The toilet-paper ball popped out of the barrel, flew high in the air, and plopped right into the toilet bowl!

The whistling, screaming, and applause continued for a full minute. The talent show was over. Kids flocked onto the stage to see the JAMPAC up close. I was laughing and jumping.

Lindermann stood in the audience and gave me a smile and a salute. I saluted back. JAMPAC was a huge success.

The Siege of Barnswall Sloo

Wave after wave of warriors had been pushed back by the villains who had shot arrows and thrown stones from atop the high walls of the castle. Although the force of men who called themselves Big Eyes was mighty, their attack on Barnswall Sloo had thus far failed. The castle was too strong.

As the sun rose high, brave knights Sir Cam and Sir Fonkiss addressed the Big Eyes.

Spake Sir Cam, "I was once inside yon castle. They have water aplenty. We shall fail at waiting for them to surrender."

"Sir Cam speaks the truth," spake Sir Fonkiss. "Our siege demands new weaponry. Look!"

Up the hill strode Prince Lynder, ruler of the Big Eyes. Behind him, pulled by many oxen, rolled a gigantic cart, covered with blue cloth.

Once the cart was positioned, Prince Lynder commanded the Big Eyes to remove the covering. Beneath it, shining white in the midday sun, rested a powerful siege engine, a device that could hurl balls of molten destruction into Barnswall Sloo.

The knights cheered!

Soon the castle would fall.

* * *

I like stories of knights and battles, so I took my imagination back in time and turned Lindermann's JAMPAC into Prince Lynder's siege engine.

You probably guessed, but just in case, I am Sir Cam and Georgie is Sir Fonkiss. I reversed our last names, kind of.

And the Big Eyes are the Big Guys. Duh.

I turned Aunt Lois's wall toilet sculpture into a castle, but it was hard to name it. So I asked my mom, and she gave me a whole bunch of strange names for toilets (lav, john, WC, can, commode, head, privy, etc.). But once she told me that in England a toilet is sometimes called a loo, then it was easy. The toilet on the wall of the Barn became Barnswall Sloo.

Oh, and this is Chapter X+ because I think they used Roman numerals when knights did sieges.

I'd have to do a lot more reading about the Middle Ages, but maybe someday I'll write a book about knights.

Chapter 11

Shorts, Snakes, and Sneaking

After the talent show, it took a long time for the guys in Cabin H to settle down and get into bed. Everyone was in a great mood. Kevin was juggling stuff, and some guys were trying to copy him. Others were begging Lindermann and me for a chance to try out the JAMPAC. Georgie, still dressed as Ee-Gorg, was shambling around, making insane noises. It would've been totally great except in the back of my thoughts, I was anxiously waiting to do the Cool Duel vote.

I guess Sam was anxiously waiting, too. Because as soon as Lindermann disappeared into the bathroom, Sam whispered loudly, "Cool Duel vote. I'll count it out. Ready . . . one, two, three."

The fists and hands went up. Alfie voted for me. Jimmy, who had been on my side on Day One but not since, came back. So did Ethan. Oddly, Danny switched back to Kevin. I thought Sam might vote this time, but he still abstained. The vote was 9–6 again.

"I can't believe you guys," Kevin muttered.

Back in my cove, I tallied the votes.

COOL DUEL DAY SIX

ME	KEVIN	
	√	Ty Atkins
√		Alfie Bickelman
	√	Lloyd Case
	√	Jason Chelsea
	√	Tommy Grace
	√	Noah Keil
√		Jimmy Kelly
√		Cheesie Mack
√		Zip Matthews
	√	Henry Miranda
		Sam Ramprakash

ME	KEVIN	
√		Ethan Rhee
	√	Clark Rosellini
√		Georgie Sinkoff
	√	Danny Stephens
	√	Kevin Welch

So close! All I needed was for Danny to switch back to me and one more. Tomorrow was the last day. I needed to think of one last cool thing to do.

Lindermann came out of the bathroom and flipped off the lights. "I'm going to the counselor meeting. I'll be back later. Behave yourselves."

As soon as our squeaky screen door closed, I heard Kevin say, "Goodbye, Ron-Nerd Lindermann. I don't even want a scary story tonight."

Of course he really does, I thought.

And that was when I knew exactly what I was going to do! I'd make up the scariest story ever. I'd think up one that would be cool enough to get me the votes I needed to win.

Scary stories need scary villains.

Like what? I lay in bed thinking:

1. My first idea was a headless horseman. But nah, I had already mentioned that.

2. *Headless* made me think of my dad and his missing foot. How about a pirate with a peg leg? Nah, I'd rather have something almost believable, something that could actually happen in camp. And I'm pretty sure there are no pirates in central Maine.

3. Instead of a peg leg, how about a villain with only one arm? Yeah! And it would not only happen in camp, the villain would be a camper.

If I could scare my cabin mates, I'd definitely get lots of Cool Duel votes. But it had to be a complete surprise. I wouldn't even tell my best friend.

I lay in my cove thinking up a One-Armed Man story. I'm sure I fell asleep with a smile on my face.

COOL DUEL DAY SEVEN

In the morning, after Uncle Bud announced "shorties all around" over the loudspeaker, I got Lindermann alone, told him my plan, and asked if he'd help me with it that evening. He loved it.

Then I overheard this conversation at the flagpole:

Kevin: But you and I have been friends forever.

Alfie: So?

Kevin: So why'd you vote for Cheesie?

Alfie: His JAMPAC machine was very cool.

Kevin: You can't do that.

Alfie: Sure I can. It's a free country.

Jimmy: Lay off him, Kevin. What you're doing is definitely *not* cool.

At breakfast Kevin was unusually quiet. I figured he was getting nervous about the Cool Duel vote. He didn't participate in any of the usual conversations. But at lunch he and Ty were whispering a lot. I was pretty sure the Cool Duel was about to heat up.

I was right.

Our afternoon activity was flag football. This was the first time we'd had it. If you've never played, it's just like touch football except every player has a flag (a rectangle of colored cloth like a handkerchief) tucked in his waistband. You "tackle" a player by grabbing his flag and holding it up. This is usually a fun game for me because of my speediness, and my really good mood got even gooder (not a real word, but you know what I mean) when Barry, the counselor in charge of flag football, named Ty and me as captains.

As a Little Guy, I used to be captain lots of times. This was a first for me as a Big Guy. Ty and I did rock-paper-scissors to see who'd go first, and I won. I chose Danny. He is an excellent passer.

Georgie gave me a strange look, like *Hey! I'm your best friend.* But I had a plan. I knew Ty hated Georgie almost as much as he hated me, so he'd never choose him, and I was trying to get guys on my team who were important to me in the Cool Duel vote.

Ty chose Kevin. Big surprise.

Now I was glad I'd tallied up the votes every night. I remembered that Lloyd, Jason, Tommy, Noah, Henry, and Clark had never voted for me once. Those were the boys I wanted on my team. And Georgie.

I chose four of them (Ty grabbed Noah) until only

Clark, Georgie, Sam, and Zip were left. I picked Clark and was totally shocked when Ty chose Georgie. Georgie gave me a see-what-happens look. I chose Sam and felt sorry for Zip since if anyone else but me had been captain, I'd've been chosen last instead of him.

We huddled up.

"Danny, you're quarterback," I said. "Who wants to hike?"

Clark raised his hand.

"Okay. Your call, Danny—what's the play?"

At first it was fun. The teams were pretty even, and we were ahead 21–14 when I faked left, cut right, and Danny tossed the football over Jimmy (he was guarding me) right into my hands. I had only Kevin to dodge. There was no one else between me and the goal line. I tried the fake again, but Kevin didn't fall for it. He reached and grabbed my shorts. An instant later they were around my knees, tripping me to the ground. Kevin picked up my flag and held it high.

Everyone laughed.

I wasn't certain he did it on purpose, so I laughed, too.

Two plays later, I caught the ball again, and this time Ty pulled my shorts down.

"My mistake," Ty said. "But I did get your flag." He picked it off the ground and held it up.

I might've been okay with this if at least one other boy got pantsed. Then it would've been a joke . . . or a new way to play flag football. But for the next forty minutes it was only me. After the fourth time, Georgie had had it.

"Come on, guys," Georgie said to Kevin and Ty. "Let's play football, not goofball!"

They ignored him, and there really wasn't much more he could do because he was on their team.

I pulled up my shorts. The score was 35–35. Barry, the counselor in charge, had been lying on the grass not paying attention throughout the game. Now he lifted his face out of his car magazine and called out, "Wrap it up! Next touchdown wins."

The ball was at midfield. We huddled up. Danny called the play: a fake to me and a pass to Jason on the other side.

"Hold on, Danny," I said. "I've got an idea."

With my butt facing the huddle so the other team couldn't see, I pulled my flag out of my waistband and tucked it under the elastic of my underwear.

"When they try to pull down—"

"Perfect!" Danny said. "Great idea. Okay, fake to Jason left. Pass to Cheesie right. On three."

We lined up. Clark bent over the ball.

"Hut! Hut! Hut!" Danny shouted.

Clark hiked the ball. I took off. Danny faded back, looking to the left at Jason streaking toward the goal line. He faked a throw to him, then turned toward me and threw a bullet. I was running at an angle toward the sideline and cut back to the middle just in time to grab the pass. Kevin was on me in a flash. He grabbed my shorts. At the exact instant he pulled down, I stopped and jumped straight up.

Touchdown!

Right out of my shorts!

My flag, still tucked in my undies, waved behind me as I sprinted for a touchdown.

I turned around to see my teammates jumping up and down and Georgie rolling on the ground laughing. We won, 42–35.

It wasn't a complete victory because just then the loudspeaker sounded wash-up-for-lunch, and Kevin retaliated (fought back) by running to the nearest tree and flinging my shorts high up onto a branch.

"You win!" he yelled as he trotted toward the cabins with the other boys.

What a bad sport. I looked up. I had never climbed a tree in my underwear before.

"You are totally going to win the Cool Duel now," Georgie said.

"You think so?" I replied, pulling myself up onto the lowest branch.

"Definitely," Georgie said. "I bet you get almost everybody's vote tonight. What could be cooler than a tighty-whitey touchdown?"

As I grabbed my shorts and started down, Georgie suddenly yelped, "Cheesie! Look!"

At the base of a nearby tree was a nest of baby garter snakes. There must have been twenty.

Neither of us is the least bit afraid of snakes, and anyway, garter snakes mostly don't bite and aren't exactly poisonous. Most snakes lay eggs, but garter snakes are born alive because the mother's eggs hatch inside her body. (I learned a lot about garter snakes from Lindermann later in the summer. If you like or hate snakes, there's more about them on my website.)

"Oh, man!" Georgie said. "We've got to show these to the guys."

We squatted and watched them wriggle for a few seconds. Then I pulled on my shorts and Georgie took off his T-shirt. We scooped up about a dozen tiny critters and wrapped them in his shirt, rolling it so none could escape.

Interesting fact: Snakes are *not* slimy.

Just before we got to the cabins, Lindermann spotted us.

"Hey, guys, I need your help dismantling the JAMPAC. I have to clear off the stage in the Barn."

"I'll be right there," Georgie said, opening our cabin door. "I gotta show the guys what we found."

Lindermann and I walked to the Barn.

(Because I was with Lindermann, I did not actually witness the bad news that happened in our cabin. Therefore, from the stars below until you see the stars again, it's Georgie doing the writing.)

* * *

Hi! I am Georgie Sinkoff writing this.

First I have to say that it was not Cheesie's fault. In fact, he didn't even know anything about it.

Here's what happened.

I went into our cabin with that bunch of baby snakes in my T-shirt. I was going to show them to everybody. But Kevin was in the bathroom and Ty was reading a comic book and not paying attention to me. So I instantly got one of my Great Ideas.

I thought it was a Great Idea that would really help Cheesie in the Cool Duel.

But my Great Idea turned out to be a Terrible Idea.

Here's what I did.

I unrolled my T-shirt on Kevin's bed.

Then Kevin came out of the bathroom. He walked to his bunk. I thought he'd freak out when he saw the whole mess of snakes. I thought he'd do something really uncool like scream like a baby or something.

But Kevin just stood there, looking right at the baby snakes.

He did not freak out.

He picked up a snake and put it over one ear. Then  he picked up another snake and put it over his other ear. Then he took another snake and scrunched it between his lip and his nose like a wiggling mustache.

Then he said, "All right, you guys. Which one of you jerks did this?"

All the kids cheered and cheered.

It was the coolest thing I will ever, in my whole life, see anyone do with snakes.

I could tell Kevin would get lots of Cool Duel votes because of this.

I told Cheesie I was really, really sorry.

* * *

"I'm really, really sorry," Georgie said to me as we hurried to meet the girls before dinner.

Georgie is my best friend, so of course I forgave him, but I was sure he was right. His Terrible Idea had definitely lost me votes.

(When Goon found out, she bragged that Kevin loves snakes. He had one as a pet when he was ten, but when it escaped into his house and was never found, his grandmother got scared and wouldn't let him get another.)

"What're you going to do?" Georgie asked me.

I didn't answer. I couldn't even tell my best friend about the One-Armed Man story.

As we neared the dining hall, I began to think about Marci and Lana. I didn't want to do the Hack anymore. I decided to tell them this would be the last one. But we were a few minutes too early, so Georgie and I waited, eating the last of the candy he'd gotten at the canteen after lunch. He held up a piece.

"Everybody knows *dud* means something that doesn't work. So why do they call these things Milk Duds?"

I had no idea, but it took my mind off my problems for a while. (I'm going to contact the Milk Duds company and ask. If I get an answer, I'll post it on my website. If I don't, I'll make one up.)

The girls arrived, and I started to head into the kitchen, but Marci motioned for Lana to speak.

"Um, okay," she said. "This is weird, but lots of the other girls said what you and Georgie did at the dance was really funny. So maybe I shouldn't have gotten so upset."

She paused like it was my turn to talk, but I didn't have anything to say.

"So," Lana continued, "I'll apologize for getting upset if you'll apologize for embarrassing me."

That was easy. "Okay," I said quickly. "I apologize." I opened the door and went into the kitchen.

Mookie and the other kitchen staff were moving

around, doing last-minute dinner prep. Tonight was pizza. Georgie wanted to snag a slice, but it wasn't ready.

"Yo, Cheeseman, you back to recalibrate the dyna-troopy system whammy?"

"Something like that," I replied.

Mookie wiped his hands on his apron. "Hey, Booth, watch that garlic bread for me, would ya?" He walked toward us. "So, why don't you tell me what you kids are really up to?"

"Huh?" I said.

"Good afternoon, ladies. Good to see ya, Georgie." He crossed his arms, sort of blocking our way to the computer room, and stared. "C'mon, talk to me straight. My cousin cued me in on your fake computer lingo."

We were busted. I looked at Marci.

"Okay. It's my brother, my twin brother. . . ."

She retold the story, and Mookie listened and nodded sympathetically.

". . . and because of his broken leg, he couldn't come to camp."

Suddenly I knew what had caused my M&M-itis. Her story was untrue. And I knew what I needed to do to prove it.

I held up my hand. Marci stopped talking. Everyone stared at me.

To them I'm sure I still looked like Ronald "Cheesie" Mack, but in my mind I had become R. Cheshire MacAronie, Esq., the world-famous lawyer who always got the truth out of those he questioned.

"Excuse me, Marci," I began. "Before camp started, did you receive a letter from Camp Leeward telling what items to bring with you?"

Marci was surprised by my question. She looked at Lana, then nodded.

"And did your brother receive a similar letter from Camp Windward?"

She nodded again.

I was setting a trap. "So, is it correct that your brother had been told he was accepted into Camp Windward?"

"Yes," Marci said softly.

"When did you say Marcus canceled coming to camp?"

When Marci didn't answer, I (Attorney MacAronie) turned away from the witness and faced the jury (Mookie, Lana, and Georgie). I waited. . . .

Finally Marci spoke. "Um . . . about . . . I don't know . . . maybe about a week before camp started."

"That is so not true," I said, turning back toward Marci.

She was speechless.

I continued. "You're as old as me and Georgie. So Marcus, your twin brother, has to be the same age. You say he canceled just before camp started? Impossible. If he did . . ."

I paused and spoke very slowly and calmly.

". . . there would've been one empty spot in the Little Guys cabin. That spot would've been available for Georgie . . . and we wouldn't have been shoved in with the Big Guys."

"Yes!" Georgie said in a loud whisper.

"You don't even have a twin brother, do you?" My cross-examination was complete.

For an instant nobody said anything. Every

member of the kitchen staff was staring at us. Then Marci ran out of the kitchen.

In a tiny voice I could barely hear, Lana said, "I'm sorry, Cheesie," and ran after her.

(Once I started writing this story, I realized I should've known a lot sooner that Marci didn't have a brother. Earlier in the summer she had said something that proved she was an only child, but I didn't catch it. Did you? The answer is on my website.)

"Okay," Mookie said, walking away. "I'm guessing the computer problems have disappeared. Time for me to make some pizza."

When I sat down at our table in the dining hall, Kevin was in a great mood, laughing and joking with everyone about the garter snakes. He even had one tucked in his T-shirt pocket. He seemed really confident. The final vote would come in a few hours. If I lost, I'd have to make a Kevin-is-the-coolest announcement and bow down to him. I would be completely humiliated. Guys would talk about it for years.

But I had one chance left.

Everything depended on the One-Armed Man.

Chapter 12

The One-Armed Man

That night's campfire was fun, and when it ended everyone was in a good mood . . . just perfect for my scary story. So as we got into our pajamas, I gave Lindermann the signal to begin.

"Listen, you guys," he said. "I know some of you have complained because I don't tell scary stories. Well, today Cheesie was in Uncle Bud's house, and he told me he read a really scary article in the newspaper."

Kevin flopped back on his bed in disgust. "Aw, c'mon! We don't want to hear some stupid newspaper junk from the Runt."

"Just give it a chance," Lindermann said. "It's Cheesie or nothing. He says it's really scary."

Georgie gave me a look that said, *How come I don't know anything about this?*

When the grumbling stopped, I began. "Today's paper had an interesting article about a crazy man who escaped from the mental hospital in Farmington. Did any of you see it?" Of course I knew they hadn't, because none of them read the newspaper, and anyway, I was making the whole thing up.

Most of the boys just stared, but a few shook their heads. "Well, from what I can tell from the article, this guy went crazy about fifteen years ago at some summer camp around here. Not this camp, though."

"Boring," Kevin muttered.

I ignored him. "He was about twelve then, because now he's in his midtwenties, the article said. Anyway, he only has one arm, and that's one of the reasons he went crazy."

"Boring," Kevin repeated more loudly.

"It seems that one night this kid—he was a well-known mischief maker—"

"Like me," Ty interrupted. Lots of kids laughed.

"He snuck out of his cabin after lights-out and

went down to the lake. He didn't take a flashlight because the moon was so bright. He got into the camp's motorboat, planning to take it out for a run. But he must've forgotten to untie one of the mooring ropes——"

"What a dope," Jimmy said.

"Because when he started the motor, the boat shot forward, jerked to a sudden stop, and threw him into the water. He came up for air just as the boat spun back at him and ripped off his arm with its whirling propeller. The last thing he saw before he blacked out was the red running lights on the motorboat."

"Motorboats don't have running lights!" Ty shouted.

"Yeah, you're right," I said. "But that's what the newspaper said. I didn't make this up."

Ty turned to Kevin. "He is *definitely* making this up."

"Hey, look," Lindermann said. "If this doesn't interest you guys, Cheesie'll just quit. We can turn the lights out and go to sleep." He looked around the room, but no one said anything else . . . so he nodded to me, and I continued.

"Okay, then. He would have drowned for sure, but one of the counselors had heard the motorboat start up and ran down to the lake just in time to see the kid get hit. He dove in and saved him. Then it was a race to see if they could get him to a hospital in time to keep him alive. I guess he was really bleeding."

"Really bleeding!" Sam was getting excited. "If you ripped an arm off, you'd bleed to death in two minutes."

"Not necessarily," Lindermann said calmly.

"Sure you would!" Jimmy shouted.

"Shut up, you guys. I want to hear this," Zip said.

I took a deep breath. "The kid went crazy because he lost his arm. At least that's what the paper said."

There was a long pause. Finally Kevin said, "So, what else?"

"That's it," I said.

"What? That stinks! That's the dumbest story I ever heard," Kevin said, plopping back onto his bed.

Lindermann stood up. "Sorry, guys, I was hoping you'd like it. Let's get ready for bed." He walked around the cabin, picking up baseball gloves and other junk and tossing them onto bunks. I went into the bathroom and got my toothbrushing stuff.

Then I hurried back out like I had just remembered something. I had my toothbrush in one hand, my toothpaste in the other, waving both. "Oh, yeah, I forgot one thing. The article said that this guy, after his stump healed, became violent, attacking anyone with two arms."

Kevin sat up. "This is totally not true!" He turned to Lindermann. "I *know* Cheesie's making this up."

Just like I had asked him to, Lindermann pretended to be mad. "Listen! You guys have asked me over and over to make up a scary ghost story. But I already told you I don't believe in that kind of juvenile stuff, didn't I?"

Lindermann leaned over Kevin's bunk and stared straight at him. "You can believe Cheesie or not . . . I don't really care." He walked slowly back to his bunk, then turned around and looked at all the kids, who were surprised that he had raised his voice.

Lindermann's outburst quieted the place down, and soon everyone except me was in bed. I just stood in the doorway to my cove.

"Is that all the newspaper said?" Georgie asked.

I paused to think, then said, "No, actually, the paper said that the police were going to look for him in the lakes around here, because he's escaped before . . . and that's where they caught him last time."

"It's dumb to put that in the paper," Ethan said. "If you wanted to catch somebody, you wouldn't go telling everyone where you planned to look. What if he reads the paper? He'll just take off to somewhere else."

Ethan looked around the room. Several boys nodded in agreement.

"Yeah, maybe," I said. "Look, I'm sure this is a stupid thing to bring up, but I don't think there's anything to worry about."

They all looked at me. Up until that moment, no one had been worrying about anything. I squeezed toothpaste onto my brush.

"What do you mean?" Georgie asked.

"There's nothing to worry about. If this crazy man really came up here to the lakes, and Ethan's probably right about him reading the newspaper and running the other way, he'd have eight or nine lakes to choose from. Why would he pick *this* lake?"

I began brushing my teeth.

"And if he did pick Bufflehead, which is really a long shot, there are six camps on this lake. There's Grand Vista, Highfield, Webster Pines, those two way over on the south side . . . so, counting us, there are *six* camps. Why would he pick this camp?"

Toothpaste foam was beginning to drool out the corners of my mouth.

"And if he happened to pick this camp—I mean, now you're really talking about the impossible—there are twenty cabins on our side, and he might go to the girls' side. And our cabin isn't closest to the lake or to the road. Why would he pick *our* cabin?"

By this time the white drool was halfway down my chin, giving me, I hoped, an eerie appearance.

"Unless"—I paused—"he came through the

woods." There was complete silence as I wiped my chin with the back of my hand. "The paper said he carries a red flashlight with him wherever he goes. It has something to do with the accident."

Sam spoke, his voice barely audible. "The lights on the motorboat!"

I waved my toothbrush at him. "I bet you're right!"

That got all the kids deep-thinking, so I disappeared into my cove.

Lindermann walked to the front door, hit the switch, and said, "Lights-out!" As he walked back to his bunk, he said softly, just like I had asked him to, "Remember how Cheesie said he attacks people with two arms?"

"Yeah, I remember." I could tell it was Zip.

"Well," Lindermann continued, "I don't know about you guys, but I'm going to sleep with both my arms under the covers tonight. I know it's silly, but let's just say I'm trying to stay on the safe side of things."

Kevin was still not convinced. "I don't believe any of this. Cheesie made it up, didn't he?"

"Good night, Kevin," Lindermann said. He waited a moment or two, then said quietly, "Arms under the covers."

Except for the usual rustling of blankets, beds, and sheets that accompanied bedtime, there was no noise. I remember thinking that the woods were strangely quiet . . . just right for my plan.

I waited fifteen minutes. I wanted my victims to be asleep.

I sat up, put on my sweatshirt, and pulled the hood down tightly. Then I put on my shoes and grabbed my flashlight—I had taped some red plastic from the crafts room over the light. I stood up on my bed and pushed at my window screen. It was hinged at the top and swung out into the night air.

I shined the red flashlight out the window. The stepladder that I had asked Lindermann to put against the wall was right where it was supposed to be. I waited, listening for any sound from inside the cabin that would indicate that someone was still awake.

Silence.

I climbed out.

Once outside on the ladder, I waited with my head still in the window, listening again to make sure no one had heard me.

Silence.

I climbed down and hid one arm inside my sweatshirt and tiptoed around the cabin, avoiding the sticks and leaves, walking soundlessly on the dirt beside the cabin. I got to the front door and opened it.

I know this sounds like a scary story itself, but that night—maybe because I opened it so slowly—our cabin's screen door squeaked like all those doors in horror movies. It made a soft, high-pitched, stuttering *scree-eech* that went straight up and down my spine.

I stepped inside. As I flashed the spooky red glow over each kid's sleeping face, I could see that every one of them had both arms tucked under the covers. Sam had his covers pulled all the way over his head.

With the empty sleeve of my sweatshirt dangling, I walked to the back of the cabin, shining my flashlight up at Lindermann's bunk. He was on one elbow, grinning at me.

It was time. I kicked one of the legs of Georgie's bed.

He opened his eyes to a world of red light.

There was a moment of nothing while Georgie's sleepy brain cranked itself up to speed. Then . . .

"HE'S HERE!" Georgie screamed in complete and total terror.

"Keep your arms under the covers!" Lindermann yelled. "KEEP YOUR ARMS UNDER THE COVERS!"

For the next minute, the cabin was a horfusing

(*horrible* plus *confusing*), conforrible (*confusing* plus *horrible*) jumble of cries, yells, and the sounds of running and crashing. Someone slammed into me and screamed. At last Lindermann climbed down and flipped on the lights. I couldn't believe my eyes.

Kevin and Henry were huddled together in a back corner of the cabin, whimpering.

Sam was standing on his bed, completely wrapped in his blanket and moaning. His nose was bleeding.

Clark and Danny were running back and forth inside the cabin, not knowing where they were going.

Several boys were missing. I guessed they had run outside.

Lloyd was the only kid still in bed, both his arms under the covers. He was wailing over and over, "I peed in my bed. I peed in my bed. I peed in my bed. . . ."

I looked for Georgie, but he was gone. After looking under his bed, I tried the bathroom. Georgie was standing in the toilet. That's right. *In the toilet!* He had dashed into the bathroom when the crazy man showed up, ducked into the stall to hide, and jumped up on the toilet seat so that his feet wouldn't show. In the darkness he had missed and landed in the bowl. I looked at him and laughed. I was still laughing when I heard Uncle Bud storm into the cabin.

"What the blue blazes is going on in here?" he shouted.

I ran out of the bathroom. Georgie, his pajama bottoms dripping, followed.

"Omigosh, Granpa. It was great! I totally terrified everyone with a scary story." I was so excited, I forgot to call him Uncle Bud.

He turned around slowly, taking in the chaos. When he saw Sam's bloody face, he pulled off a pillowcase and pressed it to Sam's nose. Then he noticed Lloyd, who had finally gotten out of his wet bed. It was obvious that he had peed his pajama bottoms. Uncle Bud looked up at the ceiling, took a very deep breath, and let it out slowly.

"Lindermann," he said wearily, "change this boy's sheets. Get your campers calmed down. And get this cabin to sleep."

Dutcher came in with Alfie, Jason, and Noah. The

boys were trembling. "What's going on? I found these guys hiding behind some trees."

Uncle Bud didn't answer. Dutcher followed him as he left the cabin.

Lindermann changed Lloyd's sheets and cleaned up Sam's nosebleed.

No one looked happy. None of the boys, including Georgie, now in dry pajamas, would look at me. Some were still shaking, and all were embarrassed.

I went into the cove, climbed into bed, and tried to figure out what had gone wrong. They had begged for a scary story, and I had given them what they asked for. But I had scared them too much. What if they had nightmares for the rest of their lives? I could still hear someone whimpering as we all tried to get back to sleep.

I had definitely overdone it.

But it really was an excellent scary story.

Just before I fell asleep I realized we had forgotten the final Cool Duel vote.

Chapter 13

The Final Vote

The next morning I awoke before the other boys and peeked out of my cove. Flag raising was at least thirty minutes away, but Lindermann was already heading out the door. I got dressed in a flash, and even though it was against the rules to leave your cabin before the flag-raising call, I ran out after him. He was sitting on a rock by the side of the cabin.

"That was some story you told," he said.

I nodded. The wake-up trumpet call sounded. "I think the kids all hate me."

Neither of us spoke for a while. Finally the flag-raising trumpet tooted and everyone came pouring out of the cabins.

Tons of kids from other cabins rushed over and surrounded my bunk mates, trying to find out what had happened. I peeked around the corner of our cabin, concerned that the guys I had frightened would still be embarrassed.

Everyone was talking at once.

"Shut up! *Shut up!*" Georgie shouted. "I'll tell you what happened. Cheesie told this super-terrific story, and—I'm not kidding—I got so scared, I jumped in the toilet!"

Everyone laughed.

"And I got so scared, I peed in my bed!" Lloyd yelled proudly.

Everyone laughed even louder.

Sam, standing on our cabin steps, jumped up and down and screamed for the whole camp to hear, "Cheesie told us the scariest story in the whole world! We've got the greatest cabin that ever, ever existed!"

Then Georgie saw me, ran over, wrapped me in a bear hug, and swung me around. "Oh my gosh, Cheesie, that was the best story you ever made up."

He put me down, grabbed my shoulders, and shook me hard. "You have to put it in your next book!"

(Which, of course, is exactly what I'm doing.)

Dutcher came up to me on the way to breakfast. "From what I've heard, I'm thinking your One-Armed Man might be better than my Zombie Attacks. How about you tell it to me sometime, so I can pull it on my campers next year?"

I was grinning ear to ear all through the meal. The dining hall was way noisier than usual. Everyone was chattering about our cabin and my story. Lots of girls stood at the Border Line, begging every nearby boy for information. I saw a grinning Goon point at me and make a thumbs-down motion. I guess she was hoping I was in trouble.

I barely had a chance to eat because kids were constantly coming over to tell me how terrific my scary story was. But what they said to me was like that game called Telephone, where you whisper something into one kid's ear, and he whispers it to another kid, and so on, so by the time it gets to the last kid, the story is completely different. According to what campers told me and what I overheard them telling each other, my bedtime story was about sharks in the lake, a one-eyed man with a hook, and poisonous red licorice (don't ask!).

Our morning activity was a nature hike in the woods with Lindermann. We were stopped in a clearing, and he was telling us about birds of prey.

". . . tremendous eyesight. From two thousand feet in the air, nearly a half mile up, an eagle can spot a mouse moving through the grass."

Then he paused.

"Hey, you know what? With all the excitement last night, you guys didn't get a chance to do your Cool Duel vote."

We all looked at each other. How did he know?

"You guys are not as sneaky as you think," Lindermann said. "And I've got very good hearing. I'm going to take my camera down to the lake, sit on that rock way over there, and see if I can snap a photo of an osprey grabbing a fish. Yell for me when you're done."

I hadn't been nervous for any of the preliminary

votes, but now, as we stood around waiting until Lindermann was out of earshot, I was *very* nervous. I really wanted to win.

"Maybe Lindermann's not such a bad guy after all," Kevin said when we could no longer see him. "Okay. Let's vote."

"Alphabetical," Sam said.

"By first names or last names?" Alfie asked.

"Last names," Zip said quickly. "It's always last names."

"Okay, then," Ty said. "Atkins. I go first. I vote Kevin."

"I'm next. I vote for Cheesie," Alfie said.

Then Lloyd, who I had scared into peeing in his bed, voted for me! That was a switch.

Then came Jason, Tommy, and Noah . . . all for Kevin.

"I vote for Cheesie," Jimmy said.

I wished I had my tally pad with me. It was going to be very close.

"That makes it four for Kevin, three for me, so far. I vote for me," I said.

"Me too," Zip said. "Not for me, I mean . . . for Cheesie."

I was ahead, 5—4!

Then Henry voted for Kevin.

Sam abstained again.

Ethan voted for me.

Clark went for Kevin.

It was now tied 6—6 with only three remaining: Georgie Sinkoff, Danny Stephens, and Kevin Welch. Since it was obvious how Georgie and Kevin would vote, everything depended on Danny.

I went over the previous tallies in my mind. Danny had switched back and forth on every vote. I had no idea what he would do now.

Georgie threw his arms in the air and shouted, "I vote for Cheesie!"

Danny looked around. "I guess it's my turn. Okay. Here's the way I see it. The whole purpose of the Cool Duel is to choose which one of these guys is the coolest in camp. Of course that's actually me, but for some reason I'm not in this election."

"Ha, ha. Not funny. Just vote," Zip said.

"So, looking at what's gone on over the last week, it's clear to me that both guys have done some very cool things. Kevin's snake face. That toilet paper launcher. Cheesie's stupid dancing. Kevin's excellent juggling. Underwear flag footb—"

"Give us a break!" Jimmy shouted.

It was clear to me that Danny knew he was the deciding vote and was stretching the whole thing out.

"Okay. All in all, I'd have to say that balancing one cool thing against the other . . . looking at everything . . . weighing the pros and cons—"

Zip grabbed Danny in a headlock. "Vote!"

Danny struggled free and grinned. "Okay. I'd say the guy who did the coolest things is . . . Cheesie—"

Georgie and a couple of other guys started to cheer. I had won!

"—but because we've been camp friends for years, I'm going to vote for Kevin."

I had lost.

"You aren't supposed to vote for friends!" Georgie shouted. "You're supposed to vote for who's coolest!"

"Quiet!" Kevin yelled. "He voted. It counts. Let's move on. I still get to vote."

The vote was only 7–7. Kevin wanted to make his victory official.

"Like Danny said, the whole purpose of the Cool Duel is to choose which one of us is the coolest guy in camp."

Now he's going to give a speech and rub it in, I thought.

"I'm definitely the coolest, of course, and Cheesie's a sawed-off runt who doesn't belong in a Big Guys cabin."

What a bad winner.

"But he ended up in our cabin, and I've got to hand it to him. He put up a great fight. That one-armed dude with the flashlight was awesome."

Huh?

"So . . . I vote for Cheesie."

I won!

I don't remember anything else that happened that day.

Long after lights-out, I lay under my blanket staring at the final Cool Duel tally.

COOL DUEL DAY SEVEN

ME	KEVIN	
	√	Ty Atkins
√		Alfie Bickelman
√		Lloyd Case
	√	Jason Chelsea
	√	Tommy Grace
	√	Noah Keil
√		Jimmy Kelly
√		Cheesie Mack
√		Zip Matthews
	√	Henry Miranda
		Sam Ramprakash

ME	KEVIN	
√		Ethan Rhee
	√	Clark Rosellini
√		Georgie Sinkoff
	√	Danny Stephens
√		Kevin Welch

In the morning, Kevin would have to announce my coolness to the whole camp and get on his knees and bow down to me. I thought I would feel triumphant, but I didn't. Kevin had completely surprised me by being a good sport. That was probably the coolest thing he had ever done. It was weird. I went to sleep with a frown.

I woke up with a smile, knowing what I had to do.

While everyone was getting dressed, I got one of the guys alone and convinced him he needed to change the way he'd voted.

Can you guess who it was and what he did?

The answer's on the next page.

Chapter 14

The Final, Final Vote

One second after the loudspeaker called everyone to flag raising, Sam announced loudly, "I am no longer abstaining. Cheesie is cool. Kevin is cool. But Kevin's voting for Cheesie makes him the coolest. I vote for Kevin. It's eight to eight. It's a tie!"

I stuck out my hand.

Kevin shook it.

And even though in the final week the Orange team (mine) lost the Color War, the rest of camp (including the second dance in the Ballroom, where Georgie and I were asked to do our crazy dance again and lots of other kids joined in) was terrific.*

---

*When we lined up to leave camp on the last day, Mookie surprised me with a birthday cake. Even with Georgie eating four slices, there was enough for every kid on our bus. It was a delicious way to end the summer.

It's a tie!

Chapter 15

Coda

I am in my room at home writing this chapter. If you know why it's called Coda, then you probably play a musical instrument. A coda is the end of a musical composition like a symphony. Meemo—who plays the violin—told me that the "chapters" of a symphony are called movements. The last movement of this story took place back home in Gloucester.

It was a phone conversation.

Lana: Hi, Cheesie.

Me: Hi.

Lana: What're you doing?

Me: Writing my book about camp.

Lana: Am I in it?

Me: Yeah.

Lana: And Marci?

Me: Yeah.

Lana: Are you still mad about the Hack?

Me: No.

Lana: 'Cause we only did it because after Marci met Georgie, she thought he was cute and really liked him.

Me: Oh.

Lana: And because I liked—

Me: My mom wants me. I gotta hang up. Bye.

After I hung up I realized there was one thing about the Hack I never understood. If there was no twin brother Marcus, who or what or why was Marci texting? If you have an idea, please go to my website and tell me.

Oh, and I forgot to tell you that Goon got really

mad and made a fool of herself when she found out Kevin and I were friends. I awarded myself four points for that, so at the end of summer camp, the Point Battle score was 669–668. With me leading!

Ha!

But now that Goon and I are in the same school, there have been lots more Point Battle events, and I'm behind again.

Ugh!

* * *

It's early November, and this is the end of *Cool in a Duel*. I hope you liked it.

I just had another adventure, and I'm going to start writing about it in ten minutes or so. It's about a mess I got into in middle school. When I have a title, it'll be on my website.

I was going to write "The End" here, but Granpa (who "accidentally" erased the lovey-dovey video I took of Goon on his camera) is looking over my shoulder, and he wants to have the last word, so here goes:

This is Bud Mack here. I have read this whole book, and except for the part that says I tell terrible jokes—which I certainly do not—everything that Cheesie wrote about camp is accurate.

And then both of us gave you, the reader, a squinty-evil-eye.

See you next book!

Signed:

Ronald "Cheesie" Mack

Ronald "Cheesie" Mack (age 11 years and 2 months)

CheesieMack.com

The End

(but keep reading anyway)

Appendix A

How the Point Battle Is Scored

These rules apply equally to Goon and to me. I do not cheat. Otherwise, why bother?

If one of us insults the other—

- When we're alone: 1 point
- When other people can hear: 2 points
- Points are doubled for a REALLY excellent insult.

If one of us causes the other to do something embarrassing—

- When we're alone: 2 points
- When other people are around: 4 points
- Points are doubled for a REALLY excellent embarrassment.

If one of us gets punished—

- By parents: 4 points
- By school: 8 points
- By police: You lose—GAME OVER

Points are doubled when . . .

- it's a REALLY BIG punishment.
- you're caught lying.
- the other kid tattles.
- the other kid is actually at fault but gets away unpunished.

Appendix B

Visit CheesieMack.com If . . .

1. You want to tell me what you think about this book. (page 6)
2. You're interested in strange names for body parts. (pages 13,31)
3. You'd like to know the rules for Georgie's and my License Plate Alphabet Race game. (page 14)
4. You want to read the report I wrote about primates. (page 24)
5. You're curious about bufflehead ducks. (page 29)
6. You want to hear how Lake Chargogga-goggmanchauggagoggchaubunagungamaugg

is pronounced. (page 29)

7. You want to read Uncle Bud's joke. (It's not very funny.) (page 51)

8. You know something about the Abominable Snowman, Yeti, Sasquatch, or Bigfoot. (page 59)

9. You want to learn how to play Roboto. (It's very cool!) (page 69)

10. You have an idea how I could finish the "Legend of Double Wobbly" story. (page 81)

11. You want to know more about lemurs. (page 86)

12. You know another "clothing" verb, like *belt, sock,* or *skirt.* (page 91)

13. You think short-sheeting is cool and want to learn how to do it. (page 108)

14. You want to see what I did in my fifth-grade robotics club. (page 113)

15. You have an addition to my list of animalish words. (page 124)

16. You want to hear a loon call. (page 139)

17. You're interested in what I learned from

Lindermann about garter snakes. (page 184)

18. You want to know why those candies are called Milk Duds. (page 188)

19. You can't figure out what Marci said that proved she did not have a twin brother. (page 192)

20. You think you know who, what, or why Marci was texting. (page 220)

21. You're curious to see if I have a title for my next book yet. (page 221)

Acknowledgments

Many, many years ago I told a scary bedtime story to a cabin full of campers. Their faces and names have escaped, but their screams of terrified delight are in this book. Thanks. I also wish to thank Dan Lazar and Jim Thomas, agent and editor, for their patience and guidance through rewrite and rewrite and . . .

YEARLING HUMOR!

Looking for more funny books to read?
Check these out!

- ❏ *Bad Girls* by Jacqueline Wilson
- ❏ Calvin Coconut: *Trouble Magnet* by Graham Salisbury
- ❏ *Don't Make Me Smile* by Barbara Park
- ❏ *Fern Verdant and the Silver Rose* by Diana Leszczynski
- ❏ *Funny Frank* by Dick King-Smith
- ❏ *Gooney Bird Greene* by Lois Lowry
- ❏ *How Tía Lola Came to ~~Visit~~ Stay* by Julia Alvarez
- ❏ *How to Save Your Tail* by Mary Hanson
- ❏ *I Was a Third Grade Science Project* by Mary Jane Auch
- ❏ *Jelly Belly* by Robert Kimmel Smith
- ❏ *Lawn Boy* by Gary Paulsen
- ❏ *Nim's Island* by Wendy Orr
- ❏ *Out of Patience* by Brian Meehl
- ❏ Shredderman: *Secret Identity* by Wendelin Van Draanen
- ❏ *Toad Rage* by Morris Gleitzman
- ❏ *A Traitor Among the Boys* by Phyllis Reynolds Naylor

Visit **www.randomhouse.com/kids** for additional reading suggestions in fantasy, adventure, mystery, and nonfiction!